CURSED WISHES

THREE WISHES HISTORICAL FANTASY BOOK 1

MARCY KENNEDY

Editor: Christopher Saylor at www.saylorediting.wordpress.com/services/

Cover Design: Damonza at https://damonza.com

Published June 2018 by Stronghold Books

Print ISBN: 978-0-9920372-1-5

ALSO BY MARCY KENNEDY

THREE WISHES SERIES

Three Wishes: A Prequel Short Story

Cursed Wishes

Stolen Wishes (coming summer 2018)

Broken Wishes (coming fall 2018)

Fallen Wishes (coming winter 2018-2019)

STANDALONE SHORT STORIES

Frozen: Two Suspenseful Short Stories

BUSY WRITER'S GUIDES

Showing and Telling in Fiction

Deep Point of View

Internal Dialogue

Description

Dialogue

Point of View in Fiction

Grammar for Fiction Writers

Fiction Genres

CHAPTER 1

(handwritten notes: "Q = question" and "Gavran POVC")

Isle of Skye, Scotland, 1501 AD

Only a madman or an *eejit* went out into a storm on the moors.

Thunder burst overhead, and Gavran Anderson instinctively ducked. He probably was a bit of both for trying to beat the storm, but the wolves or the weather would be the death of his missing ewe if he left her out here. And it was his fault she'd been left behind in the first place.

If he'd been able to sleep even one night through without the dream, he might not have miscounted the sheep when he drove them in. It seemed he must have done something to anger the Almighty. Or the fae. Why else would he be cursed with the same dream, every night repeating, like a fiddler who could play only one song? He'd begun to feel as if his mind weren't his own.

He turned off the narrow cattle path and trekked uphill into the gale, measuring his steps through clusters of jagged rocks. His dadaidh swore before he set out that the ewe was a lost cause, and that Gavran's time afore the storm hit would be better spent laying the framework for his new home. His wedding was planned for month after next.

Dig your bait while the tide is out, his dadaidh said. *You've no notion of what the morrow will bring.*

Madness though it might be, he wasn't going home without his ewe. Whatever the morrow brought, he bore the guilt if they lost the ewe and, with her, the lamb this spring and meat or barter come fall. Leaving the ewe for dead stole food from his family's mouths. He'd seen too many times in their neighbors that sometimes a single poorly timed loss meant the difference between prosperity and starvation. He'd not let his family become one of the latter because of a mistake he'd made.

He hoisted himself up onto the flat rock at the top of the peak and turned in a circle on its platform. The storm's gusting wind yanked at his clothes, and thunder rattled his chest. No ewe as far as he could see.

Time played against him. The landscape looked like night drew in even though the sun rested high in the sky. Once the rain came and blinded him, it'd end his search.

A new cascade of lighting lit the bruise-colored sky, and the form of a bird careened against the backdrop of the charcoal clouds.

He shouldn't linger on high ground.

Another flash drew his gaze back to the bird. There were two this time, looping in the pattern of vultures waiting for something to die. They might have found nothing more than a rabbit carcass, but they might have found his missing ewe.

His hands ached from clenching his fists. He splayed his fingers in a stretch and shook out his grip. The sooner he faced whatever they circled, the sooner he could return home. Maybe he'd even beat the heart of the storm.

He skirted down the opposite side of the hill from where he'd ascended. The vultures swooped over the dry river bed, near the end where a long-ago rock slide dammed it off from the water's main flow.

Once on the flat, he broke into a jog. He skidded to a stop at the ledge.

A lump too large to be his ewe lay crumpled on the cracked ground at the bottom of the gorge. The wind licked up the edge of a cloak the color of wood left exposed to the elements for too many years. He caught a glimpse of the body beneath. No man'd be that frail. It had to be a woman or child whose bones the vultures were eager to pick.

He crouched and slid down the bank. Rocks and loose dirt cascaded in front of him. Halfway down, a small ledge stopped his descent, and he picked his way down the rest of the drop at an angle. The figure didn't stir.

The reek of the fly-covered vomit next to the body choked him. He gulped air in through his mouth, but the taste lingered on the back of his tongue, and he fought down bile. This would be a simpleton's errand if he'd come all this way to find only a rotted corpse. But if the person had already passed, the vultures would be feasting, not flying. The person must still live.

He squatted and rolled the body over. A woman—tangled, rust-colored hair matted around her face. A gash split the sleeve of her leine from elbow to wrist, and the hem of her skirt was frayed beyond saving, revealing ankles thin enough to snap with one hand. Her feet were bare and bloodied.

The next burst of light highlighted skin blackened by dirt and bruises. The woman's eyes were closed, and she dragged in rasping breaths.

She still lived, but not for long if the storm caught her out in the open in such a condition. How did a woman come to be lying here, alone, so near to having the Cù-Sìth arrive for her soul?

The roaring sound of a heavy downpour rushed toward them.

They were out of time.

He'd risk both their necks to climb back up the steep bank with over seven stone of dead weight on his back, but the river gorge traveled half a day's walk before leveling out into a gentler slope.

Many would tell him not to risk his life for a woman who seemed to be flirting with the hereafter already, but he refused to be the same man in life as he was in his cursed dream. He didn't abandon the innocent.

3rd Day ; ✶

He knelt, grabbed the woman under her arms, and rolled her forward, chest down, over his shoulder.

Black clouds sank and hunched near to the ground. No time to take the long route. He picked his way up the embankment diagonally. With each step, he dug in his toes, then breathed. Dug his toes, then breathed.

✶ The first drop of rain splattered on his brow. He had to reach the top before the rain turned the slope into slick mud. He gulped in two lungfuls of air and lunged the final steps. He hit the grassy flat and stumbled to one knee.

The clouds opened up. Rain soaked through to his skin and drenched the woman's clothing, adding more weight. She twisted in his hold but showed no other sign of coming awake. Escaping the storm would be much easier if she could at least stand on her feet. She convulsed again.

A knot grew in his stomach, and he clutched her legs tighter. He couldn't carry her if she kept flailing. He sang the words of a ballad into the wind—the song his sisters begged for when they were little and couldn't sleep. Perhaps this woman's soul would hear him and take peace from it even if her mind couldn't.

She stilled on his shoulder, and he struggled to his feet.

Lightning burned across the sky, so near the stench of scorched air filled his nose, and the thunder threatened to crush him with its weight.

They'd not make it home before lightning fried them both.

He'd be wiser to wait it out in the abandoned Campbell cottage the next croft over.

He stepped over the low-lying stone fence that hadn't been patched since the Campbells left when he was a lad and ducked his head against the rain lashing his face. The cottage crouched ahead of him in the haze, as if it didn't want to be found. The daub of clay and straw had crumbled away from the thin oak branches woven behind it to create the walls, and the reed roof had collapsed in the back like a sinkhole.

He shouldered the sagging door open and lowered the woman to the dirt floor. He sank down beside her and rested his head back onto the wall. Mud soaked through his cloak and trews to his skin, and drops of rain dripped from the roof, barely missing his feet.

Exhaustion seeped through his body along with the wetness. He'd rest for a moment to catch his breath before seeking to find what ailed the woman. They wouldn't stay dry, but at least they'd be safe until the storm passed...

His chin dipped to his chest, and he jolted awake.

Christ defend him. With the dreams keeping him up at night, he couldn't even stay awake during a storm that might well blow the cottage in on top of him. And with a near-dead woman to care for. A bead of sweat joined the rain running down his temple.

He couldn't bear the dream, the sleepless nights, much longer without going mad.

Ragged breathing rattled the woman's twitching form. He wasn't a healer like his mamaidh, but he could check if a sickness or broken ribs caused her labored breaths.

He wiped his clammy palm on the chest of his wet leine and touched her forehead. He jerked back. Her skin burned like cooking coals.

Her eyes fluttered open.

Lightning shattered the darkness with a boom that made his ears ache. She stared up at him with brown eyes that didn't seem to see him.

A beat harder and deeper than the thunder shocked his heart. He recognized her eyes. The dying woman on the floor in front of him was the woman from his dreams.

CHAPTER 2

Gavaran POVC

She couldn't be the woman from his dreams. His mind played him false. A dream was but a dream. Only bairns still believed their nightmares were real after waking, and he was a man of five and twenty.

He leaned in closer. With pale skin and high cheekbones that would crinkle her eyes if she smiled, she looked like enough to the woman in his dream to be her changeling. Perhaps his mind used her face to fill in the gaps. He could never bring the woman in his dreams into focus.

That must be it. It was a passing resemblance. Nothing more.

Or maybe it went the other way. Maybe he had met her before as a boy, and his mind had created the dream woman from a faded memory of her. Just because his dream borrowed a piece of reality didn't mean the rest of it had to be true as well.

"Do we know each other?" he asked.

Her eyes rolled back, and her lids fluttered closed.

His hands trembled like he'd been hit with a palsy. Despite the reasonable explanation he'd come up with, a tiny voice in his head chanted for him to run.

Run and not look back. Run and leave her behind. No one would know he'd found her. No one would know he'd left her. Bringing home a woman who looked so much like the one in his dreams could only bring trouble down upon his head.

A deep cough bucked the woman's body.

He rocked back on his heels, putting more distance between them and shrinking the distance between him and the door. Leaving her here condemned her to death, but taking her with him wasn't necessarily the right thing to do, either. If she had a catching sickness, bringing her home would place his family at risk.

Nae, that was an excuse. He knew it as sure as he knew his own name. He could send Finnegan and his sisters away before he brought the woman near, protecting them. His mamaidh would gladly take the risk the same as she did when she went to minister to the needs of any who fell sick.

He wasn't the same man in life as he was in his dream. He wasn't a coward. He wasn't selfish. He'd not allow a woman to suffer if he had the power to save her.

He whipped off his cloak, wrapped it around the woman, and drew her back into his arms. The roof had stopped dripping, so the storm had likely passed. He needed to take advantage of this

break while they had it. The weather on the isle changed in
a blink.

He stepped out into a light drizzle. The sun chased at the
clouds.

He crossed to the sheep path, now a sludge trail of manure
and mud. He waded through the grass on the edge instead.

A wave of dizziness unlike anything he'd felt before shoved
him sideways. Her sickness couldn't have passed to him so
quickly. The dizziness had to be because he hadn't eaten anything
since the night's meal day before. When he left at sun-up, he
hadn't planned to be gone so long.

All he needed was a moment's rest.

He sank to the ground and cradled the woman in his lap.
Even unconscious, her body seemed to curl into him like a child
starved for human touch. The stench of sweat and rot leached
from her, and his stomach turned over. Maybe it was best he had
an empty stomach after all.

He forced himself up again and trudged the final mile home.

His dadaidh pushed a barrow filled with dirt across the soggy
turf by the house. "Some ewe."

Gavran shrugged his unburdened shoulder. "She's deathly
sick. Best send the others to the Nicols' before I near in case it's
catching."

"I'll send the lasses away with the bairn." His dadaidh lowered
the barrow. "But your mamaidh won't go, seeing as the priest's
come again. You'll need her help with the care anyway."

The now-familiar tension that accompanied every one of his mamaidh's attempts to purge him of the nightly dream slid up Gavran's spine and fused it into a rod. If it weren't for the woman in his arms, he'd turn back and spend the night in the Campbell cottage rather than listen to the priest prod him to confess whatever secret sin the dreams were retribution for. If he could free himself of the dreams by a simple confession, he'd have done it long ago.

His dadaidh disappeared into the house, and moments later, Morna and Ros set off through the field, a bundle that must be Finnegan tucked in Morna's arms.

His dadaidh came out after them and retrieved his barrow. "Since the ground's too muddy now for much else, I'll take a look for your ewe."

The way his dadaidh glanced back over his shoulder toward the house made Gavran think he'd been looking for an excuse to escape until the priest was gone. Like as not, he suspected why the man of God had come again, and all talk of Gavran's dreams made his dadaidh want to plug his ears and hum a tune.

Gavran carried the woman inside. The smoldering fire in the center of the house filled the room with smoke and the heavy smell of wet ash. When the rains came strong enough and at the right slant, nothing could keep them out.

His mamaidh and the priest rose to their feet on the far side of the table.

Gavran laid the woman on his straw tic. Her skin had a

greyish tint where raindrops had washed away the grime. She looked so fragile, as if she should have blown from his hold on the walk back. "I found her on the moor. I don't know what ails her."

The priest set aside his mug. "I'll have a look. There's fair little I haven't seen before."

Gavran sacrificed his place at her side to the priest and pulled his mamaidh to the farthest corner of the house. "Strange time for clergy to pay us a visit." He kept his voice low.

She gave him her you-might-be-a-grown-man-but-I'm-still-your-mamaidh glare. "You've bags under your eyes big enough for a grouse to nest in."

Facing an inquisition was supposed to help him sleep better? He crossed his arms over his chest.

His mamaidh sighed as if she could read his thoughts. "If it's not punishment for a sin, then it's an evil spirit beyond my skills to drive away." She patted his cheek. "If you've no care for your health, you should at least care for your soul."

He'd already tried everything she'd suggested, from turning his clothes inside out, to wearing a pouch full of St John's wort and red verbena round his neck at night. The dreams continued. So far, the priest hadn't proved any more successful. He'd begun to think the dream was his version of St. Paul's thorn in the flesh, given to keep him humble.

The seductive rhythm of phrases recited in Latin hit Gavran's ears. He spun around. The priest leaned over the woman. The death words and what-a-pity-you-die-so-young-and-all-alone tone sent a chill across Gavran's shoulders and down his arms.

He stumbled across the room. The woman's chest still rose and fell, rattling on the exhale like a loose wagon wheel. She wasn't dead yet.

The priest touched a thumbprint of anointing oil to her lips and spoke the words again. He pressed his thumb to the top of his vial to repeat, passing her from the land of the living to that of the dead.

Gavran stuck out his arm and blocked the priest's path. The priest's eyebrows shot up, perching at a reproving angle made all the more severe by his bald head.

Gavran yanked his arm back. The lack of sleep must be wearing on him more than he thought. No man in his right mind interfered with a man of God administering last rites, yet letting him go on with the ritual felt like giving up on her. Giving up on her seemed like giving up on the dream woman all over again. "Pray for her healing instead."

"I can pray for her healing, but we still need to prepare her soul for death."

He hadn't fought for the dream woman the way he should have. He wouldn't repeat that mistake now, either. "She's not dying this day."

"You can't deny her this. She can't perform penance and needs forgiveness of her sins before passing."

"She's not dying this day." He placed what he hoped was a soothing yet firm hand on the priest's shoulder. "We're grateful for your coming, but you'd best be on your way while the weather holds."

The priest sputtered a string of incoherent words.

Gavran lifted him from his kneeling position by one elbow and nudged him out the door. "I promise we'll send for you again if you're needed for unction."

His mamaidh pressed her three middle fingers into the space between her eyes. When she looked up, her face wore the same look she used to give him as a little boy when he accidentally tromped dung through the house. "Are you off your head? Removing a man of God from our home by force isn't like yourself."

His gut clenched. It wasn't like him, and it'd be on him now if her soul stayed trapped between here and the afterlife. That was almost a fate worse than what he'd done to the woman in his dream. At least the dream woman would be free of her curse upon death. "I'll prop her up so she breathes easier. Will you help me get some broth into her and brew a poultice for her chest?"

His mamaidh pursed her lips and huffed deep in her throat, but heaped wood on top of the coals and hauled a pot full of water over the growing flames. She poured a mug of broth. "Best not tell your dadaidh about how the priest left. He's already fretting Tavish will learn of your dreams and refuse to let ya marry Brighde. No need to add to it."

He'd had the dreams as long as he could remember, but anymore it seemed the dreams were the master and he was the slave—endure them, hide the truth about them, let them dictate every move he made.

Brighde would find out about the dreams after she married him. There'd be no hiding them then. Somehow it didn't sit right to allow her to go in blinded. The dreams could well drive him mad someday. Someday soon. His whole life had started to feel wrong. Unbalanced.

He crawled onto the straw tic, slid an arm beneath the woman, and pulled her up to rest against his chest. Her head lolled back onto his shoulder, and her labored breathing eased.

It all felt wrong except for this.

Holding her this way felt familiar and comfortable. "Does she look like anyone we know?"

His mamaidh lowered to the ground next to them. Both her knees cracked. She rubbed at the left one, then placed her thumb on the woman's chin and eased her mouth open. "If she's from round here, I'd like to whip the *eejit* who let her go out alone so sick and no meat on her."

She hadn't directly answered his question, but she had continued to minister to the woman while she replied. His mamaidh had never been a skilled liar. When she tried, she had to stop whatever else she was doing to focus on the lie, which inevitably gave her away. Even an indirect deception froze her body in place.

His mamaidh didn't recognize her, and she knew every member of every family in the kirk.

He tucked the woman closer. The bones of her spine and shoulder blades dug into him. She couldn't be the woman from his dream because that woman didn't exist, but something about the situation still felt off to him—a woman alone, sick in a ravine, who made him think of the woman in his dream.

Maybe she'd be able to explain it all away if he could speak to her. But to do that, he first had to ensure she lived.

CHAPTER 3

Ceana Campbell POVC

Ceana Campbell wasn't dead. Again. The ache in her
body assured her of that.

Why had she thought this time would be
different from the others? She knew better by now than to
expect to receive what she wanted. The wishes would never
allow it.

A sharp beam of light cut across her chest from the shuttered
window above, and she brushed her fingers over the solid
wattle-and-daub wall next to her. The hands that built this one
had taken great care to smooth the mixture of clay, sand, and
straw flat over the lattice of wooden strips beneath.

Wherever she was, it wasn't her family's cottage, where she'd
been headed. At the best of times, her dadaidh's construction
work looked more like someone threw handfuls of slop against a
briar patch.

Her last memory was collapsing while crossing the dry ravine, her lungs full of so much pain when she drew a breath that she'd been convinced she'd finally be freed from this cursed existence. Someone must have found her and tended her, not realizing they did her no favor.

She dragged in a breath full of the scent of boiling oats and turnips, and her mouth watered. The coziness of it reminded her why warm, cooked food tasted so much better than cold, raw food.

She should leave before the people who lived here returned.

With one palm pressed against the wall, she eased herself into a sitting position and pushed to her feet. Her legs felt like cattails bending in the wind, and she slumped against the wall.

Leaving would be more difficult than she thought. She should have known that, if she decided to stay, they'd ask her to leave, and because she'd decided to leave, her body would force her to stay. She closed her eyes.

When she opened them again, Gavran's mamaidh stood in the middle of the room, a wooden spoon in one hand.

Ceana's chest felt like it collapsed in on itself, crushing what remained of her heart.

It couldn't be.

The woman moved her back onto the straw tic. "Easy now. You've been sleeping for near three days."

The voice belonged to Davina Anderson as well, and she watched Ceana with eyes the same loch blue as Gavran's.

Ceana's hands trembled. However she'd gotten here, she needed out. Before Gavran returned. She'd promised herself that she wouldn't allow the wishes to make her see him again. It was the one promise she'd made herself.

Until this moment, she'd thought it was the one promise the wishes would allow her to keep.

"I can't ask you to care for me any longer." Her voice ground out in a bullfrog croak.

"*Havers.*" Davina folded a scratchy woolen blanket up under her chin like she swaddled a bairn. "Now that you're awake, I'll help you bathe. I can't tell if we've patched all your ills 'til we rid you of the grime."

In the time pre-wishes, Davina'd played nursemaid to the entire kirk. That seemed to remain unchanged.

She'd have to try another path if she wanted to escape. One the wishes were less likely to anticipate.

Ceana wiggled one arm out from under the blanket and pushed it down away from her face. "I can't repay you for any of this."

Davina waved her hand in the air and stirred the two large pots over the fire.

Of course, not money, either. The Andersons had been known for their generosity, too. But Davina had also been as superstitious a woman as she was a devote one. "Won't a bath only bring me more sickness?"

Davina snorted. "If you ask me, that's an excuse made by men too lazy to haul water." She disappeared out the door.

Ceana glanced back at the light flooding in the window. The windows were too small to climb out—a protective measure against people climbing in—and that left her only the front door as a means of escape. She wasn't going to waste time seeing if she could come up with a better plan. Davina wouldn't be gone long.

She clambered to her feet again and stumbled back into the wall. Her head pounded, and the room bent around her like an image under rough water. The wish that doomed her to receiving the opposite of whatever she wanted seemed to read her heart as easily as a priest read the Holy Scriptures. Wisdom said to accept her fate and return to the bed, but if she did, she wouldn't be able to avoid Gavran.

She stepped away from the wall. Her legs collapsed, and she bashed her palms on the dirt floor. She grit her teeth and dragged herself forward on shaking arms, past the table.

The cottage door swung open.

Davina rushed to her side. She scooped her off the ground and into a chair and wrapped her in the blanket again. "I would've helped you as soon as the men fetched the trough. Be still now."

Gavran and Allan Anderson maneuvered a wooden water trough through the narrow doorway behind Davina.

Davina pointed toward the fire. "Put it down there. We don't need her catching a chill again."

Gavran's gaze locked on Ceana, and his mouth drooped open slightly in the way that used to make her want to kiss it.

Now it made her feel like he was gloating over her.

Maybe she should have felt happy—or, at least, happy for them. If she couldn't have felt happy for them, she should have felt some noble sense of satisfaction surely. Her sacrifice was responsible for their prosperity. She'd accomplished what she'd set out to do. They were safe.

Barring that, she should have definitely felt something marginally ignoble like pride. The fairy had wanted things the other way around, and she'd been quick enough in her thinking to spare Gavran and take the worst for herself.

Instead she felt as bitter and filled with rage as she had when she'd given up her small portion of food to her little brother and her dadaidh snapped it up out of the boy's hands and ate it himself.

The same sense that she'd been played and had no way of rectifying it.

Of all the cruelty the wishes inflicted on her—

"Watch yourself!" Allan dropped his end of the trough with a thunk. "Are ye trying to knock me into the fire?"

Gavran's attention snapped back to his dadaidh, and he lowered his end of the trough.

Ceana rocked back and forth in the chair. She'd bathe because she couldn't escape until she had, but she'd find some way to make them want her gone. Surely that would work.

Davina draped the trough with cloth. The men returned with buckets of water and dumped them into the makeshift tub. Davina poured the pot of boiled water from the side of the fire into the trough and shooed the men from the building.

She held out her arms. "Let me help you out of those clothes."

Ceana wobbled to her feet. Davina motioned for her to raise her arms above her head and tugged her leine off, then helped her into the trough. The water funneled in around Ceana, the same temperature as early summer runoff. Not quite warm, but not exactly cold, either. Her skin pimpled.

Davina shifted around behind her.

Ceana held still enough that the water didn't even ripple. She wouldn't allow herself to lean back and hide the rows of scars given by the farmer whose apples she stole last summer when muddy water no longer tricked her stomach into believing she'd eaten. Those scars ought to be enough to start Davina thinking about whether she'd been wise to insist Ceana stay.

Davina sloshed water over Ceana's back as if no scars existed. "I ought to know what you're called. I'm named Davina. Davina Anderson. The two you saw earlier were my eldest son, Gavran, and my husband, Allan."

"Ceana." Davina might recognize her family name. That might be enough to allow her to leave if Davina thought she had kin to go to. They might even take her there themselves. "Ceana Campbell."

"Were you headed to the Campbell cottage, then, expecting to find family?"

She couldn't tell Davina she hoped to find her parents and brother. It would only lead to more questions she couldn't answer. "My aunt and uncle."

"The Campbell cottage has been abandoned since Gavran wasn't much more than a bairn."

Why didn't you know?

Even though Davina didn't speak the question, it hung in the air. The hole in her story. In the history she remembered, her family would have still been there. In the history altered by the wishes, she had no way of knowing when or why they left.

Behind her, the cloth splashed into the water again. "Are you running from someone, Ceana Campbell? If there'll be a husband or a dadaidh beating on our door in the night, I want to know."

"Nae." A pang built in her gut, pinching like it pulled little bits of her away. As soon as her three wishes took effect, she'd been erased. Left in the world, but with no history and gone from the memories of everyone she'd ever known. "There's no one. They were the only family I had left."

Davina *hmm*ed and scrubbed at her back.

Ceana rested her arms on the side of the trough, bent forward, and let her eyes drift shut. It'd been so long since she'd been touched with kindness. She wanted it to last. Which meant it couldn't. Maybe she shouldn't try to grasp it for a few seconds

—it'd only hurt more when it was wrenched away—but she couldn't seem to help herself.

Fingers brushed her wrist, and she jerked upright. Davina held her palm, facing up. The scars on her wrist from where she'd tried to kill herself eight weeks ago glared stark and ugly against her pale skin.

No good Christian home would want her around once they knew she'd sinned by trying to take her own life.

She stared straight ahead. A griddle propped against the wall beside the fire pit, in her line of sight, mocked her. Davina used to cook her oatcakes sweetened with apple sauce when she'd come here to hide from her dadaidh after he'd drunk too much mead and his words turned cruel.

Ceana licked her cracked lips, but no long-ago taste of apple lingered. This had been her safe place once. The place she'd run to. The adopted family she'd loved as her own. She never could have predicted it'd become the place she needed to run from.

She bit back the urge to curse. Her wishes had more tentacles than an octopus. "Not every life is worth living."

"True enough." Davina stroked a thumb—bump, bump, bump—over the ridges. "I can't see much worth in living life as a drunkard, a murderer, or a thief, hurting others for your own benefit."

"I've been a thief."

The words sprang out before she could stop them. Best they were out anyway. She wouldn't change course now. Better to leave, leave before leaving would add another crack to her soul she could never hope to mend.

Davina released her wrist. She cocked an eyebrow, looking even more like Gavran. "The Almighty sees the motives behind our acts, not only the acts themselves."

Ceana turned her face away. That was the cruelest twist of the wishes. She'd try to steal food and be caught, her body eating itself to survive, until she reached the point where she wanted to die. Then the wishes yanked her back, forcing her to take just enough food, just enough of whatever she needed to keep her alive. She couldn't die any more than she could truly live.

Davina tilted Ceana's head back and poured the remaining half bucket of water over her hair. She stepped away and held up a blanket. "Wrap yourself, and I'll find you clothes. With two half-grown girls, we should have something that'll fit you."

Now that part of her wanted to stay, the wishes should kick her out any second. "I can't take your daughters' clothes. I'll wash mine."

Davina made a *tsk*ing sound. "The hand that gives is the hand that gets, my husband always says. And your clothes weren't worth saving. I've already had the men burn them."

Ceana donned the clean clothes Davina left hanging by the fire. She buried her hands in the still-warm material, and her throat squeezed shut. Every small kindness might as well be a knife between her ribs. Curse Gavran and the wishes for this more than anything else. Better she never experience anything good again than that she be teased with it to have it ripped away.

She tightened the drawstring at the waist of the skirt. It fit loose even when drawn, though she suspected it was because she made a stick bug look fat rather than the girl who owned the clothes was large. Both Ros and Morna had been naturally slender when she'd known them.

A longing to hug Ros and Morna one more time spread through her. In the pre-wishes timeline, when Davina destroyed her knee and she'd been unable to walk for near a year without help, Ceana used to come every day after finishing her chores at home to cook and clean at the Andersons'. Ros and Morna had been too young at the time to handle it all themselves. She'd half-raised Gavran's sisters.

She pushed the memories aside. No sense in torturing herself with thoughts of what was.

"Now sit, and I'll make you up a bowl," Davina said. "You missed the morning meal, and I'd rather feed you up some than starve you until evening."

Ceana dropped onto the bench that butted up to the rough-hewn table. The moment when this all shattered around her had to come soon. The wishes had never held off on torturing her this long before.

Davina scooped her out a bowl of oats and added what had to be some of the last apple left over from the year before.

Ceana dug out a taste small enough for a toddler and waited

for the wishes to react—to make it taste like ash, or choke her, or cause her to break out in a rash. To make Davina yank the bowl back from her or for one of the table legs to snap and send the bowl crashing to the floor.

None of it happened. Instead, her tiny mouthful simply tasted like the applesauce oat cakes Davina used to make her.

Ceana gobbled down the rest before the wishes could catch up with her and then stared down into the empty bowl. Maybe she should lick it clean. It'd be a long time before she tasted anything this good again.

A peel of thunder rumbled outside, and she jerked. Her hand bumped the bowl, sending it wobbling in a circle and careening off the table. She reached out, wanting to stop it but not actually expecting to be able to grab it in time, but her fingers closed around it.

Her mind ground on the image of the bowl held in her hand the same as it would have if she'd looked at her reflection in a pond and it'd been a stranger staring back at her.

She shouldn't have been able to catch the bowl in time. In fact, she shouldn't have been able to eat the meal and enjoy it in the first place. Too much had gone right.

Something was very, very wrong.

If she thought fast enough, she could sometimes get out in front of the wishes for a second or two, but they never took a day of rest. They didn't take a minute of rest. By their nature, they had to prevent her from experiencing any happiness or success because she'd wished those for Gavran, and she was cursed to receive the opposite of what she'd given to him.

Her heart felt like it bumped into her ribs. The wishes couldn't have suddenly vanished, so that left only one logical explanation. When she and Gavran were together the success she'd wished for him and the failure she'd taken on herself cancelled each other out and gave them the same odds as anyone else at succeeding.

If her suspicion proved true, she had to find a way to convince Gavran that the dreams were real so that he would help her find her brother.

CHAPTER 4

Ceana picked up the *sgian* from where Davina left it on the table, next to the half-peeled turnips, and glanced over her shoulder. Davina had gone to fill the cooking pot with water, which should give her enough time. Gavran worked across the yard, near the sheep fold. Close enough to test her theory.

Everything pointed toward the wishes and curses cancelling each other out. In the past five days since she'd been awake, she'd eaten and drank, been warm and well-treated, but they'd mainly kept her resting. She wouldn't wager what remained of her sanity on a fluke caused by confinement to bed.

She ran her thumb over the smooth antler of the *sgian*'s handle and turned the six-inch blade so it reflected the light. She needed to actively test her theory before she'd be willing to risk believing it.

A shiver traced its way over her skin. The last time she'd held a *sgian*, it'd been to take her life. With this *sgian*, perhaps she could reclaim it instead.

She sucked in a breath and picked up an unpeeled turnip.

She wanted to peel it.

She repeated the words over in her mind and set the sharp edge of the blade to the turnip's skin. She cut off the head, then the root, and finally slid the *sgian* down the sides until only the white flesh remained.

She licked her lips slowly, the moist turnip resting in the palm of her hand. She'd done it. No one had stopped her. She hadn't dropped the turnip and been magically unable to find it again. She hadn't sliced off a finger, making it impossible to continue.

She had to try something else.

She laid the *sgian* and turnip on the table and climbed up after them. "I want to walk from one end of the table to the other without falling off."

She couldn't ignore the hesitation that still lingered in her voice.

"I'm going to walk across this table without falling off." She put force behind the words this time.

Four steps carried her to the end. The temptation to leap to the ground burned through her, but she wasn't fool enough to test the Almighty with a show of pride. She slid to the ground.

She indulged in a twirl. Being near Gavran did hold the effects of the wishes at bay.

Maybe her life didn't need to be forfeit. She could check on her brother with Gavran's help and then return to the Andersons'. All she'd need to do was live out her days close enough to Gavran. He owed her that much at least. And she'd learn to tolerate his presence the same way one grew used to the stench of pig manure if it meant finding peace.

She picked up the turnip again and rolled it from hand to hand. A smile tugged at her mouth. One more just for fun. Just because she could. She'd throw the turnip out the door.

She heaved the turnip with all her strength. It flew straight out.

"Ooph," a male voice exclaimed.

Gavran stepped into the doorway, dirty turnip in one hand and his other hand rubbing a red mark above his eyebrow. "Were you angry at me or the neep?"

The push-pull she'd felt around him every time since waking froze her in place and threatened to tear her apart. She couldn't quite forget that she loved him once. She'd also never be able to forgive him for what he'd done.

She couldn't even seek revenge now to try to purge the anger from her system. She needed him.

Gall seared the bottom of her throat. Even when they were bound, the wishes found new ways to torment her.

The Andersons' dogs broke into a racket of barks that turned into welcoming yips. Gavran tossed the turnip into a bucket by the door and stepped back outside.

Ceana tamped down her feelings. She had to curry favor for now at least, until she could convince him of the debt he owed her. She joined Gavran outside. A wagon bounced along the rough dirt track towards the house.

She shaded her eyes against the heavy sun. A tall man with a beard that reminded her of a bear with mange drove the wagon, and three young women rode in the back. The sun cast their faces into too much shadow to recognize any of them.

"Are these your sisters returning?"

He nodded.

"Who brings them?"

"Our neighbors." He glanced sideways at her and scrubbed his hands over the stubble on his face. "My betrothed, Brighde, and her dadaidh."

WATCHING BRIGHDE PULL UP IN A WAGON WHILE THE ENIGMATIC Ceana Campbell stood next to him felt like a new nightmare. His mamaidh hadn't left her alone for more than a minute at a time, giving him no opportunity to question her about whether they might have met before. Even though Ceana hadn't mentioned knowing any of them, being around her felt like meeting a person he recognized but whose name he'd forgotten.

Ceana swayed beside him.

Gavran cupped her elbow, steadying her. "You ought to have stayed inside."

Her skin quivered beneath his fingers like a horse shaking off a fly. "I'm alright."

She glanced at where he touched her, and her upper lip contracted. He pulled his hand away.

The wagon creaked to a stop in front of them, and Ros and Morna scrambled out. They sprinted for the house, and he and Ceana parted. The girls dashed between them, casting Ceana curious looks as they passed.

Brighde stayed seated, his eight-month-old brother cradled in her arms.

Tavish tipped his head to Ceana, then to Gavran. "Glad it wasn't the Death or influenza."

"No more than were we." Gavran strode forward and rested his hand on the wagon next to where Brighde sat. She gave him the look he waited for each time they met—the one that made him feel like he could do no wrong. The look that vowed he could learn to love her the way she loved him, given time. The look that was the opposite of how Ceana Campbell looked at him when he touched her arm. "Tavish and Brighde Nicol, this is Ceana Campbell."

Brighde doled out a smile, tight at the edges. "Campbell? I thought the Campbell cottage lay empty."

"It does." Ceana's voice was soft and flat. "But I didn't know as much when I set out. I would have died on the moors had it not been for Gavran's help."

For a second, he considered smiling at her. But didn't. "I did as our Lord commands."

"The Almighty is pleased to work through the hands of his servants," Brighde said.

Gavran cringed internally and glanced sidelong at Ceana. He'd heard Brighde make such reverent statements before, but somehow, this time, it sounded hollow.

Ceana shifted beside him. "I doubt the Almighty cares whether I live or die. At least I've seen very little of His mercy of late."

Brighde sucked in her lips until they vanished. The smile that returned to her face looked chiseled in stone and painted on, fake as the statues in the church and as fake as her words a moment before.

She extended the bundle in her arms toward Ceana. "Will you hold Finn while I climb down?"

Ceana pressed a hand into her belly and stutter-stepped backward. "Nae. I should lend a hand to preparing the evening meal."

She backed up another step and careened toward the house faster than was wise for someone who'd been confined to bed but days ago.

Brighde's eyebrows raised near to her hairline.

Gavran held back a flinch and opened his arms for Finn. "I'll take him."

Brighde handed him down and hopped over the edge of the wagon. Tavish led the horse away.

Gavran pulled aside the light blanket Brighde had wrapped around Finn. Finn's lips fluttered in his sleep. He gave him back to Brighde. He wasn't usually at a loss for words around her, but after Ceana's abrupt exit, no normal greeting seemed to fit. "Would you come inside? Mamaidh will be glad to have you both stay for the meal."

Brighde's gaze remained fixed on the path of Ceana's retreat. "She's recovered well?"

He didn't see a point in pretending not to know which *she* Brighde meant. "Aye. Well enough. Mamaidh insists she still needs rest."

Brighde fiddled with Finn's blanket, smoothing it, crinkling it, smoothing it again. "How long do you expect her to stay?"

He was no great interpreter of any woman's thoughts, but the ground beneath his feet suddenly felt ready to slide away off the edge of a cliff. "We don't know as yet. Since she's no family to speak of, my mamaidh's invited her to stay as long as she likes."

The muscle in Brighde's eye that only twitched at the end of a long day spasmed. "No family to speak of? Didn't she come to the old Campbell cottage to be with family?"

"I certainly don't know where the Campbells went."

"Then why doesn't she go back to where she came from?" Finn squirmed in her arms, and she jiggled him and snuggled him to her chest. "Hasn't anyone asked her these things? Didn't you ask how she came here?"

His ran his tongue around the parched inside of his mouth. Seems he couldn't do right by any woman today, Brighde included. He touched the spot where Ceana's turnip smashed into his face. At least Brighde wasn't throwing things at him. Yet. "I understand she walked."

Brighde's eyes opened a little too wide. "No woman walks alone to the home of people who haven't lived there in years. Where did she stay before then?"

His mamaidh believed she'd been orphaned, forced to live on her own with all that meant for a woman, and had come looking for the only family she knew of, but to find them gone. The right thing to do was to make her welcome and put her past behind like the Lord did with the prostitute who washed his feet with tears.

He doubted that answer would satisfy Brighde anymore than his earlier ones.

She puffed out her cheeks. "You can't tell me something doesn't seem off to you."

"She's no harm being here."

"You don't know that." Brighde's words snapped out. "Why wouldn't she hold Finn?"

"Perhaps she felt too weak and feared dropping him."

"Then she could have said so 'stead of running for the house." She pressed a hand to his bicep. "I'll not sleep sound at night knowing she's in the house with Finn and your sisters. You don't know one thing about her."

Lines etched in her forehead, and her eye twitched again. Brighde could be possessive of his attention, but he'd never known her to be outright unkind. Then again, he'd also never seen her in such an unusual situation before.

"Just because we don't know her doesn't mean she's a danger."

"Doesn't mean she's not, either." Her gaze darted to the door again. "And by the time you find out for sure, it'll be too late."

Brighde wasn't wrong, but if he sent Ceana away, he'd have no chance to further investigate whether some past meeting with her had incited his dreams. If he could explain them, perhaps he could also drive them away. And even if she proved not to be the woman who inspired his dream, it seemed more wrong than right to turn her out. "And what do you expect us to do, then? Send her back to the Campbells' cottage? There's not even a full roof."

"We give alms for the poor to the kirk. Surely the priest will know how to help her. Probably better than your family."

That option sat in his stomach as well as a plate of rotten vegetables. "With the meager harvest last season, I'm sure the kirk has enough mouths to feed without us adding another."

Brighde's hand tightened into talons on his arm. "I'm asking you to trust in me. Something's not right. The way she looks at you isn't right."

Was that what lay at the bottom of this? He laid his hand over Brighde's and gave her his best smile. "You've no reason to be jealous."

"Ack." Brighde yanked her hand away. "I'm not jealous. I'm scared for your life. She looks at you like she'd like to cut your throat and leave you for dead."

He knew his jaw had gone slack, his mouth hanging open, but he couldn't seem to make it close.

In moments when he caught Ceana looking at him, she didn't look like a woman grateful to or infatuated with the man who saved her. She looked at him the way he would look at an adder in his home, with caution and cunning, waiting for the right moment to chop off its head.

And with his wedding fast approaching, perhaps he needed to put aside his wain notions that Ceana might hold the secret to his dream and respect the woman who'd soon pledge to be his wife.

"I'll speak to my mamaidh. Ceana Campbell might indeed be better somewhere her family can find her should they come looking."

CHAPTER 5

Ceana paced the length of the cottage and back again. Everyone had scattered after the evening meal, leaving their bowls abandoned and the room filled with nothing but the roasted-nut-and-sweaty-feet smell of over-cooked neeps.

And her. Alone.

Dread settled in her gut, hard and cold and mean, telling her all the reasons she was a fool. She grabbed her mug of ale from the table and swigged it down, trying to drown it out.

She had to regain control of her mind. This was what over a year of living under the curse-side of her wishes did to a person. Nothing was going to go wrong this time. Gavran's family had welcomed her and cared for her.

The last few days proved being near Gavran canceled out the wishes. She could be normal again. Perhaps in time she could even be happy again. No doubt she would once she saw her brother healthy. Everything she'd suffered would still be worth it if she could see him living the life a young man his age should.

Ceana peeked out the door, but the yard lay empty except for one of the dogs gnawing on an old branch. She shouldn't allow this worry to grind at her mind the way the dog did the wood. They'd explained they planned to walk to the new site of the home Gavran and Brighde would share. That they hadn't invited her could be easily explained away. They felt she was still too weak. They couldn't know she felt better than she had in a year's time.

But during the meal, Brighde sat with her back straight as a broom handle, and Gavran refused to look at either of them. Davina ate not two bites of her meal—Ceana finished her bowl after everyone left—and the men had the same conversation about the weather affecting the crops three times over.

Only Gavran's sisters seemed at all themselves. They'd been chattering on about their favorite wildflowers, and she'd promised to teach them to make dandelion chains. It was something she'd done with them in her pre-wishes life, and with her erased from their past, no one else had taught them.

She headed in the direction they'd all gone. It wouldn't hurt anything to find Gavran and reassure herself that the added complication of Brighde had simply unsettled her.

She ought to have guessed the *love* her wishes gave Gavran would be Brighde. Brighde, who'd mooned after him since they were girls. Brighde, who'd hated Ceana for her friendship with Gavran. Brighde, whose beauty always made Ceana feel as desirable as a goat with three legs and buck teeth.

Ceana skirted the sheep fold. The sheep milled about aimlessly inside. The sun-warmed urine stung her eyes, and raised voices reached her ears. She edged a little closer, staying hidden behind the supporting beam of the lean-to.

Gavran and Davina faced off on the other side.

"Do you want me to tell her?" Gavran asked.

Davina folded her hands, extended her forefingers into a steeple, and tapped them against her lips. She shook her head without lowering her hands. "I'm the one asked her to stay. I'm the one should ask her to go."

Ceana gulped in air, but it felt as if her chest cavity had sprung a leak. It had to be a mistake. They couldn't be talking of putting her out. Not with Gavran's presence holding the wishes in check. She hadn't done anything wrong...except for the turnip incident, but surely that wasn't enough to turn her out after Davina brushed away her scars and her past.

Davina scrubbed invisible dirt from the front of her skirt. "I'll tell your dadaidh to ready the wagon and take her to the kirk on the morrow."

"And if she asks why?"

"I'll tell her there'll be no room once Brighde moves in and that the house you're building won't be ready in time. It's true enough with the way you've dawdled over the work."

Ceana closed her eyes and pressed her knuckles into her lips. She couldn't let them send her away. She wouldn't. Once they took her away from him, she'd never find her way back. Not now that she wanted to.

And he was her only hope of seeing her brother. Her only hope of anything.

She looked up at where Gavran and Davina had been. Davina was gone, and Gavran strode toward the sheep fold, pitchfork in hand.

Ceana stepped from behind the beam. Gavran stopped so suddenly he looked like he might topple over.

In a way, maybe this was all for the best. It forced her to be brave. She couldn't delay under the guise of finding the right way to tell him the way she had pre-wishes when she'd spent years trying to figure out how to tell him she loved him. She'd ended up never telling him. This kept her from doing the same thing again and losing the opportunity to find her brother.

She inched closer. "You know me. We have met before."

His grip on the pitchfork handle convulsed. The color drained from his knuckles.

Did he think she meant to attack him? With what? Her bony hands against his muscle and pitchfork tines? She was no fae with supernatural powers.

She pushed her hands forward, palms up. "We were friends once."

"You were 'dropping from the eaves." Gavran's lips thinned

into a dividing line. "You've no need to weave lies. It won't change anything."

"It's truth." A perverse desire to laugh leapt inside her. His whole life was a lie she'd created. The only true thing in it was her. She wrestled the laugh back to the ground. He'd only think her mad if she let it loose. "I've good reasons why you can't let them send me away."

It was the delay in his response, the quick look away, the rapid blinks. How his chin tucked in a fraction, almost imperceptibly.

He'd been the one to suggest sending her away.

The realization hit her like a physical blow before she could brace herself. She stepped back, unsure of where to clutch to stem the pain. A physical blow would have been more merciful. At least she could have tended the wound.

"I know you must fear being alone again," he said, "but if we take you to the kirk, you may still find your family."

He spoke the words in that slightly desperate, higher-than-normal tone that betrayed him by saying *I'm trying to convince myself as much as I'm trying to convince you.*

He'd accused her of lying. She'd combat it with the baldest of truths. "They're not looking for me. To them, I don't exist."

His shoulders dipped forward, and he leaned the pitchfork against the fence's top rail. "If you confessed to the priest whatever it is that made them cast you out, I'm sure he'd intercede for you."

Spoken with even less conviction than before.

She squeezed her eyes shut. Light burst on the backs. It was progress, however small. She had to be not only brave, but also patient, and remember that anyone would find this hard to believe.

Unfortunately, patience hadn't been one of her strengths even before the wishes. Her mamaidh had always told her that, if she didn't develop some, the Almighty would find a way to grow it in her that she wouldn't like. Of all the times for her to be right, it had to be in this.

"I gave up my family when I wished for you to always find happiness. The fairy said you'd never be happy if you remembered me, so she erased me. I exist without ever having existed. For everyone. My family included."

Gavran's face paled so much that blue circles appeared under his eyes. He slumped against the sheep fence next to his pitchfork.

She crossed the distance between them. "You keep dreaming the same dream because it happened. We were near to drowning. A fairy pulled us from the water and forced me to make three wishes on threat of throwing us back into the water to die. And one of us had to receive the opposite of whatever the other received. I took the curses and gave you the blessings."

He fisted one hand and rubbed his forefinger knuckle with his thumb in jerking strokes. "You haven't said anything you couldn't have learned from eavesdropping at another time. How do I know you're telling the truth?"

Be patient, she repeated to herself. She needed to be patient but a little longer and not lose her temper. What would he have held back? "You would have let me drown that night."

"I told my mamaidh that." He shouldered past her and marched towards the house. "We'll take you to the kirk in Dunvegan on the morrow."

"Nae." She scrambled after him and grabbed his sleeve. "I need to stay with you. When we're together, the blessing on you and the curse on me cancel each other. Staying with you is the only way I can..."

He was looking at her with revulsion, like every person who'd ever caught her stealing looked at her. It shouldn't have still hurt.

He pulled his sleeve from her grasp. "I'm to marry Brighde. If you're hunting a husband, you'll find easier men to trick in Dunvegan."

She wanted to spit on his feet, on his face. She'd given him Brighde with her wish that he'd find love that would remain true. After everything she'd given up, after everything she'd done, he still chose to believe she spoke lies. Success had stolen away the things that once made her love him. "I wouldn't marry you if you begged. I've no desire to share your bed, only your land."

"No woman will abide another hanging 'round her husband."

"You owe me."

"I owe you nothing. I saved your life that day on the moors, at risk of my own."

"I wanted to die."

Her raised voice echoed loudly off the hills and back. She clapped a hand over her mouth. Surely all his family, and Brighde and Tavish as well, had heard. She didn't so much mind his family hearing her confession, but not Brighde. She couldn't bear the thought of Brighde seeing the full extent of her shame.

Pressure filled her head, and she touched her fingertips to the line above her eyebrows. "It's not the first time I've tried. I've eaten poison mushrooms and shoved my hand into a nest of adders. This past winter I walked out onto the ice, praying I'd fall through, only to find myself back on the shore. I couldn't end my life because I wanted to, and I couldn't find a way to want to live enough that I'd finally be able to die."

Gavran laid a hand on her shoulder. She forced herself to stay still under his touch even though everything inside her curled away. If she'd finally gotten through, she couldn't risk offending him.

"You need more help than we can give," Gavran said. "The priest will—"

She stepped out of his reach. "*Eejit.*"

His arm fell to his side like dead weight.

Maybe she'd asked too much. It'd be enough to get half of

what she'd hoped for. The most important half. "At least take me to find my brother. That's all I wanted when you found me."

Wrinkles cragged Gavran's forehead. "What do you mean?"

"I didn't take the curse just for you. My brother." She couldn't keep her voice from cracking. She hadn't confided in Gavran when she'd loved him about what she'd done to her brother. She wasn't about to do it now that she'd as soon see him dead. "My brother's life would have been a better one without me in it. So I chose to save not only you, but him as well. I thought he'd be at the old Campbell cottage with my parents. That's where we used to live."

Gavran's brows lowered, darkening his eyes. "I thought you said your family wouldn't know you anymore. Why try to find your brother?"

Tears pressed so hard against her eyes that they filled her head and down into her chest. But she would not—would *not*—cry in front of him. "Not to talk to him. He wouldn't know me now. I only wanted to see that he's well and happy. It would make what I'd lost worth it." She stretched out a hand to Gavran. "If you'll take me to find him, I won't ask to stay with you. Just take me to find him."

Gavran stepped out of her reach. "I can't."

He strode away from her again.

If he wouldn't do it for her, perhaps he'd do it for himself. She ran after him. "I'm your only hope of ending the dreams."

Gavran's back went rigid.

"You haven't had them since I've been here, have you?"

So slowly he hardly seemed to move, he turned to face her. His mouth hung open enough to tell her she was right. It'd only been a guess that, since the dream had been her third wish, it'd vanish as well when they were together.

"I gave you those dreams," she said.

A woman's gasp erupted from the left.

Ceana and Gavran both spun towards it. Brighde, Tavish, and Davina stood beyond the fold, no doubt drawn by their raised voices.

Davina's lip curled. "Brighde was right. She *is* a witch."

CHAPTER 6

All of the muscles in Gavran's body that had been tightening until it felt like they'd snap relaxed. If Ceana was a witch, then nothing she said was true. The dream hadn't happened. He owed her no debt.

"What's going on here?" Tavish roared the words. They echoed off the hills like Ceana's yelled admission, but with the power of thunder.

Gavran's mamaidh chaffed her hands up and down her skirt. "Gavran's been having the same dream every night. I've been saying something unnatural caused it. And now the girl admits to being behind it all."

Tavish's face turned sunburn red. "You mean he's cursed. Were you going to tell us this before he wed my daughter?"

"He's not cursed," Ceana said. "He's blessed."

She spoke so softly Gavran wasn't sure anyone other than him heard, until Brighde whirled on Ceana.

"Shouldn't we do something about her?" Brighde's face was crinkled like a withered crab apple. "Bind and blindfold her before she bewitches us all."

Tavish stalked forward. "Grab her arm, Gavran."

Ceana backed away, her hands up. But she didn't look at Tavish. She stared straight at Gavran. "If you'd just let me explain."

"Gavran!" Tavish yelled. "Now!"

His feet seemed to have grown roots. He couldn't do what Tavish asked.

Tavish clasped Ceana's arm and twisted it behind her. He pushed her ahead of him.

Ceana looked back over her shoulder, her eyes wide, as if she couldn't believe what was happening. Couldn't believe he was letting it happen. "Gavran, please. You know I'm not a witch. You know I'm telling the truth."

Tavish bent Ceana's arm up, and she cried out. Gavran took a step after them, but his mamaidh blocked his path. She placed a hand on his shoulder and shook her head.

Ceana continued to cry his name until his ears threatened to explode.

Ros's and Morna's heads peeked out from behind a grove of trees.

His mamaidh spun on them. "Morna, take Finnegan inside. Ros, go find your dadaidh. And don't dally."

The girls scattered in opposite directions. Tears streamed down Brighde's face, and his mamaidh nudged him toward the house.

He trudged forward. It all seemed less real than his dream.

He dropped onto the bench next to the table, ignoring Morna's mosquito-like questions. Brighde sat across from him and shot glances from underneath her eyelashes. Almost as if she were afraid. Of him.

He smashed his fist on the table. It shimmied, and Brighde jumped. Morna's sentence trailed off.

Course she was afraid of him. She thought he'd been cursed.

His dadaidh returned with Ros.

His mamaidh grabbed two wicker baskets and shoved them at the girls. "Both of you go fetch some spring herbs. And don't come back 'til you hear me call for you."

They went out, and Tavish ducked inside, too tall to walk through the door frame when standing straight. "I bound her and locked her in the shed."

"We can't leave her there to starve." His dadaidh scratched his brow with the back of his knuckles, leaving a dusty smear. "I'm not one to be cruel, even to a witch."

The world had erupted with people telling him things but no one offering any proof. They wagered too much to hang decisions on either the word of a potentially crazy woman or the panicked reactions of his family. Ceana's fate on the one hand and everything he thought he knew about his life on the other. "We don't know for certain she's a witch."

Brighde burst into tears again. "Your defense proves it."

Tavish collected her into his arms. Her harsh sobs filled the room. No one else spoke.

Gavran clutched the edge of the bench with both hands to keep from stuffing a wad of cloth into her mouth. This wasn't about her. It wasn't about whether the thought of him being cursed frightened her. The truth mattered. "You've taken my words and warped them. I'm not defending her. But it might be she's not be in her right mind rather than a witch. We can't drown her or burn her at the stake for being off her head."

"How…how would she know about your dreams?" Brighde hiccupped. "You didn't tell *me* about them. How could *she* know?"

His mamaidh compulsively stacked the dishes from the evening meal. "She's been here near a week. She could've overheard."

Gavran tried to run through each barb Ceana threw at him. Had they talked about everything she said in the past week?

He gouged his nails into the wood. He couldn't remember. Maybe. Maybe not.

He hadn't told anyone she looked like the woman in his dreams. The chances of her making a guess that she looked enough like the woman in his dreams to pass for her were slimmer than taming a fox. Which meant she couldn't just be crazy. She either was right or she was a witch.

He got up and stared out the doorway at the shed. If she spoke true, he'd have abandoned her not once, but twice. He'd be honor-bound to help her.

Tavish patted Brighde's back one more time and straightened on the bench. "Which brings us back to what we do with her? Allan's right. We can't leave her bound up in the shed. If she's not a witch, we'll be guilty of murder."

"She claimed responsibility for causing his dreams." Gavran's mamaidh massaged her bad leg. "I say we take her to the kirk as planned. Let them try her and decide. Then it's in the hands of the Almighty. If she's a witch, they'll judge her heart and put her to death for her crime."

***

GAVRAN WOKE UP REACHING FOR A DREAM WOMAN WHO WASN'T there. Except, this time, she wore Ceana's face.

He swiped the sweat from his brow with his sleeve. It was the first time since he found Ceana that he'd had the dream. It was also the first night she wasn't on his family's croft. His dadaidh and Tavish had loaded her into the back of the wagon and set out for Dunvegan immediately, unwilling to keep her around him another night.

So at least that part of what she'd said was true. Having her around stopped the dreams.

He rolled onto his other side. True or not, it didn't prove she wasn't a witch.

But what if she wasn't? What motivation would a witch have for cursing him to dream the same dream every night? And wouldn't a witch have been able to escape when Tavish bound her and locked her in the shed?

Besides, it seemed that a witch's power should have been greater when she was nearer to him. His dreams should have strengthened with her around and weakened the farther away she went.

He tossed the blanket aside, hunched over his knees, and buried his face in his hands. He had a good life. He was respected. Happy.

If he allowed what she said to be true, all that might change. If he went after her and brought her back—if he could even convince them to allow it—it could jeopardize the welfare of his family. If her wishes were what kept them fed and healthy, he wouldn't be sacrificing only his own happiness in bringing her back.

Yet it said something about him if he didn't, if he let the woman who gave up her happiness for his be tried and potentially executed as a witch. If he wouldn't do the small thing she asked in helping her find her brother.

He also had no guarantee that the dreams would stop upon

her death. They might continue every night until he died as well. Or went mad. Though, if enduring the dream was the price for keeping his family safe and well, he'd find a way to survive it.

He slid from his bed. She'd said she would be satisfied if she could see her brother. His debt to her would be paid if he did that much for her. He didn't need to bring her back here and put his family at risk.

If the dream were true, Ceana made the choice to take the curse side of the wishes on herself. He might not have stopped her, but he hadn't forced her, either. As his dadaidh would say, whoever burns his backside must himself sit on it. He shouldn't be held responsible to pay for a choice she made.

Now he'd repeat those arguments to himself until he believed them.

He tiptoed across the room. No one slept by the fire tonight. Ros and Morna huddled together in bed with Brighde and his mamaidh, too frightened of being cursed by a witch themselves to separate.

He tugged on his boots. His mamaidh would worry when she woke and found him gone, but telling her he was leaving was spoiling for a fight.

He slipped outside. His dadaidh and Tavish would have camped for the night around sunset. By the position of the moon, he still had four hours until first light. That should be enough time to catch them before they broke camp, even though he chased them on foot. They didn't own a horse, and he'd never been much of a rider anyway. He'd make it faster on foot than if he got himself thrown and broke his neck with a borrowed mount.

He set off at a jog on the rutted wagon path toward Dunvegan.

GAVRAN DREW UP SHARPLY AND DOUBLED OVER. CROSSING THE boundary was like having the source of his energy sucked out of him. His body seemed to weigh twice as much.

It could have been his imagination. He'd slept maybe three hours this night.

But something inside him knew it wasn't. He'd felt a similar sensation the morning he'd been out searching for his lost sheep, before he found Ceana. He'd attributed it to fatigue and the weather then. Now he knew. He'd crossed whatever the line was between being away from Ceana and with her. The benefits of the wishes were gone. He was a normal man.

He spotted the wagon with the horse hobbled beside. The men's snores rumbled from the wagon bed. With the wishes held in check, he wouldn't have them helping him convince his dadaidh and Tavish to take Ceana to find her family rather than ferrying her to the kirk.

He slunk forward. He didn't want to wake them until he had a chance to ask Ceana a few questions. Just because he'd felt strange when he came close to her didn't mean that wasn't another trick of hers. He needed more evidence before turning his family against him, even if for a short time.

They'd tied her sitting up to a tree on the far side of the clearing, as far from them as possible while still keeping her in sight. He skirted around, staying to the tree line, and came in behind her. Her blindfolded head slumped forward on her chest, and her chest strained against the ropes, as if her bones had abandoned her body and with them all her strength to hold herself up.

He touched her shoulder. She jerked, and he clamped his hand over her mouth.

"It's me," he whispered in her ear.

He eased his hand away and removed the blindfold. She glared at him, her eyes narrowed into accusing slits. It made her face look even thinner than before. And more helpless.

He knelt down into the grass beside her. The dew wet his trews, and a chill crawled up his legs. "If you want me to believe you and help you find your brother, you have to answer my questions."

A muscle twitched in her cheek, and for a second, he thought she might refuse. Then she nodded once. The hatred in her eyes could have frozen the ocean.

"What were the wishes you made?" he asked.

"You know that already." She spat the words out.

He batted his hands in a *shh-shh* motion. "Humor me. You say my dream was real. Well, I want to check some details."

"I wished that you would find love and that that love would always remain true." Her voice tore on the last word. "I wished that you would be spared pain and only face success and happiness."

So far she'd gotten them both right. Her words were almost identical to the ones spoken by the woman in his dreams. But there was one more. The one he could never understand. "And the final wish?"

"That every night you'd dream of me and what happened."

The air rushed from his lungs like someone had trod on them. "Now I want to know why you wished the dream on me."

A cloud crossed the moon and blacked out her face. When it shone again, she'd turned away from him. "I told you why that night."

"The dream is imperfect. Like pieces are missing."

The vein beneath her temple pulsed. She muttered something he couldn't catch.

"What did you say?"

She drew in a shuddering breath. "I should have been more precise in my wish. I knew I couldn't trust her to have it turn out the way I'd tried for unless I was specific, but I couldn't think clearly."

She squirmed within the ropes, her heels digging for purchase in the dirt.

He wanted to brush back the hair that fell across her face, but he didn't. "So why the third wish? You could have wished for anything. Why that?"

"The fairy, she told me you wouldn't remember me, that no one would. I'm no great loss from the world." A smile warped her lips, then died prematurely. "But I needed someone somewhere to know I existed and that I did something worthwhile. That for that one moment, my life mattered."

Her words burrowed deep inside, and his heart beat a strange rhythm. He knew he'd never told anyone that the woman in his dreams was out on the sand bar collecting cockles the night they almost drowned because she was attempting to prove her worth to her dadaidh. Or how he somehow knew the dream woman felt valueless.

Ceana stared at him, her face devoid of emotion. "Is there anything else?"

"Just one thing." The question that plagued him. "Why you?"

Her face tightened. "*Why me* what?"

"Why did the fairy choose you? Choose us?"

"I don't know."

She spoke with the ease and even tone of someone telling the truth, but it didn't make sense.

"There must be some reason. Fae don't show up without warning to rescue drowning—" He almost said *couples*, but he didn't know what they were before the wishes. "Drowning people for no reason, and then force them to make wishes for one of them to get the opposite of what the other wishes for."

"If your help depends on me having an answer," she said in a tone that clearly said *I'm done trying to convince you*, "then go home."

He rocked back on his haunches. If she'd created this, made up the dream and bewitched him, she'd have had a good answer for him. Everything else held together too well for her to have missed that detail. She could have said she'd stolen something from the fairy or crossed her in some other way. She hadn't. Instead of proving her story false, that mystery made him more certain of the truth.

He stood and brushed off his knees. "I'll wake them and tell them we need to find your brother."

"They won't listen. They'll only think I've bewitched you again."

She had a point. They were more likely to tie him up as well to keep him out of the way until they'd left her and brought him safely home again. Especially given he'd pursued them out here in the middle of the night.

He pulled his *sgian* from its hiding spot high on his left side and sawed through the rope binding her. "If we go now, we'll be well ahead before they wake. I'll return home once we've found your brother."

CHAPTER 7

The raw skin on Ceana's wrists where she'd been bound burned. She stared at the loose rope. "You're going to take me to find my family?"

Gavran pulled her to her feet. "We have to go now if we're going. They'll look for you as soon as they wake."

The sky was already lighter than when he'd first woken her, all streaks of orange and crimson. The men could rise any moment.

She followed Gavran back through the trees. Maybe she should ask him what changed his mind. She knew better than to trust him. But opportunities didn't linger for the hesitant. They favored those who chased them. And she couldn't be worse off for following him now than she had been bound to the tree. At least she was free.

He moved a low-hanging branch out of the way for her.

"Where would your family have gone when they abandoned your cottage?"

She looped the rope around her waist and tied it off. "I have no idea."

He stopped, and she plowed into him.

He rubbed the front of one foot against the heel of the other where she'd stepped on him. "You said you wanted me to help find your brother. I thought that meant you knew where he might be."

"You assumed." As much as she'd explained the wishes to him, he still didn't seem to grasp the extent of what they meant. "How would I know? Nothing I do has succeeded in the year I've been under the wishes."

Gavran slapped his palm against a tree trunk. "We need to figure this out before we go any farther."

"You said yourself your dadaidh'll be after us as soon as they wake." She made a shooing motion with her hands. "We can't stand here and make it simple for them."

"And if we run off in the wrong direction, they'll catch us when we double back."

It was easy for him to be so optimistic about their chances of staying hidden long enough to make a plan. He knew only success. She tugged on a tree branch, testing to see if it would hold her weight. It didn't budge. She hoisted herself up so her stomach rested on the branch and swung her legs over. She tested the next branch.

"What are you doing?" Gavran asked, his head now level with her shoulders.

"You can fiddle around down here waiting for them to catch you, but I'm going to find a safer spot to think on where my family might be."

She swung up onto the next branch. A scuffling noise below told her Gavran followed suit. It was almost like they were children again, climbing trees to reach the fruit at the top.

When she couldn't see the ground anymore for the leaves, she stopped. Now they'd have some cover when the men woke.

Gavran settled in on a branch below and to her left. A holler broke the morning stillness, and sparrows shot into the air above the clearing.

She tried to keep an I-told-you-so look from her face, but she wasn't sure she succeeded. It felt wonderful to be right, to have something go right. She might as well savor the feeling while it lasted. As soon as they found her brother and Gavran went home, she'd be back to the way things were.

She wrapped her arms around the trunk and leaned close to Gavran so that, even if the men came near where they hid, they wouldn't hear her. She hoped. "My dadaidh had a cousin in Dunvegan. Her husband was a thatcher. He always said there was more work for him in town, so like as not they're still there. Whether or not I exist shouldn't have changed that, and they might know where my family is."

Gavran cocked his head, and she strained her ears, listening for voices or branches breaking down below.

Gavran slid down to a lower branch. "I think they've headed off."

She scurried down after him.

They left the cover of the trees, cut off perpendicular to the road until it was out of sight, and set across an open field for easier walking.

Gavran glanced at her sidelong with a hesitancy in his eyes that she hadn't seen before. "Why did you think your brother's life would be better if you hadn't existed?"

She should have known he'd come back to that eventually. The Gavran she knew never forgot a fact about anyone he met. But she didn't want his pity or, worse, to have his pity turn to disgust. "I need your help, and you owe me a debt. Let's leave it there."

The expression on his face might have been regret, but she focused on the ground at her feet rather than looking at him long enough to figure it out.

They walked the rest of the way to Dunvegan in silence, stopping only to eat strawberries she spotted along the path. She was accustomed to ignoring her stomach. The cramping in her gut and unpleasant taste in her mouth took some getting used to, but she'd discovered ways to turn her mind away from it. She didn't envy Gavran the sensation, especially when he'd never known real hunger.

The sun sank into the water, casting Dunvegan Castle to the north into murky shadows, as they entered the cluster of two-story homes and shops comprising the town. The pigs who wandered the streets during the day to clear away some of the rubbish had already been brought in for the night. Ebbs of weak candlelight filtered out of the cracks around the doors and from windows of the wooden houses like fingers of an evil fae grasping at their ankles.

Goose pimples popped out on her skin, and she wrapped her arms around her middle. They might not have to worry about evil fae, but she knew from experience that other evil beings roamed the streets at night. "Best not to still be here after curfew."

"Which way?" Gavran asked.

She led him through the maze-like paths between the buildings. Even if they weren't in the same house, someone there might remember them or know them and be able to direct them to the right spot.

Their hovel looked exactly the way she remembered it. Same door that looked like it couldn't support its own weight, and a roof that the thatcher never had the time or materials to fix for himself.

Gavran marched up to the door, but she drew back. For the first time since the wishes, she sent up an actual prayer. If her family happened to be here now, she'd glimpse her brother's face this night.

Gavran banged on the door. A woman answered.

Ceana tucked in behind Gavran and blinked twice to be sure her eyes didn't play her false.

It was her dadaidh's cousin, but unlike the house, she'd changed. The skin hung from her in folds like wax that had melted down the side of a candle and congealed again. Her lip was cracked, and her clothes looked patched one too many times over, the original material long gone.

Ceana's tongue dissolved into the bottom of her mouth and disappeared. She tapped Gavran's elbow.

He greeted her dadaidh's cousin. "We're looking for Irving Campbell."

"He's not here." The woman inched the door closed a little more. "And I ain't paying his debts no more. If you want money, you'll have to find him."

Ceana rubbed her hand over her forehead. Some things never changed no matter how many fairy wishes came along, and it seemed her dadaidh still welched on work and ran up debts he couldn't pay. A snake couldn't change its scales. Except without her around to care for things, the burden had fallen to others.

Though her brother should have stepped up to the responsibilities she'd left instead of allowing their dadaidh's poor choices to hurt others.

Gavran glanced back at her and lifted his eyebrows as if to say *what now?*

She crept up beside him. "We're not after money. I'm...a friend of his wife. Do you know where they might have gone?"

"You're awful young to be a friend of Agnes, aren't you?"

Ceana chewed the inside of her cheek. If she still thought they were after her dadaidh for money, she wasn't likely to tell them where her mamaidh and brother were. "She helped our mamaidh when she was so sick. Our mamaidh passed this winter and wanted us to bring Agnes a few items as thanks."

The woman's face drooped into fresh folds. "Aye, that kindness sounds like Agnes. I fear I have sad news for you."

She opened the door a little wider. Ceana glimpsed a sheep lipping the straw from the torn side of a straw tic long in need of replacing.

"Her son wasn't right," the woman said. "And when my worthless cousin found out, he left her and the boy. She tried to provide for him, but even with what help we could give 'em, Agnes died of a sickness in her lungs last winter."

Ceana's knees buckled. Gavran caught her before she hit the ground.

It didn't make sense. Her cousin must be thinking of someone else. Her mamaidh couldn't be dead, and her brother couldn't still be addled in his brain.

Her body wanted to continue to lean on Gavran, but she forced her legs to straighten and support her own weight. "What do you mean, their boy wasn't right?"

The woman tapped her head. "Up here. Even when he was

ten, he wasn't any further along than my littlest one, and she were only five. Didn't get no better as he grew."

Brilliant white and black spots blossomed in Ceana's vision.

"What happened to the boy?" Gavran asked from a distance.

"Ran off soon as the weather turned warm. My husband was too harsh on him if you ask me." The woman shrugged. "Haven't seen him since."

It was a lie. Or a mistake. "You're wrong."

The woman's expression closed down, all compassion gone from her face. "I've got things to do. Be on your way now."

She slammed the door in their faces. Ceana surged forward and beat on the door. Gavran grabbed her around the waist and spun her away. She flailed against his grip.

It wasn't supposed to be this way. She'd been the one who hadn't kept a good enough watch on him when they were little. She was the reason he fell from his cradle as a toddler learning to climb things. She was the reason he hit his head and didn't have more smarts than a bairn no matter how old he grew. With her gone, he should have been normal, healthy.

But he was worse off than before and so was her mamaidh. She was dead, and he was as good as. With the brains of a child, how could he hope to survive long on his own?

She sank to the ground. "It was all for naught."

All she wanted was to lie down and never move again, to let the ground swallow her up so she could forget. Almighty forgive her for thinking it, even hell would be preferable if she could only forget. She was too tired to think.

She was so heavy, unbearably heavy. The pounding in her head. The air couldn't find its way down her throat. Not enough air.

Steady arms lifted her from the muddy ground, and the seal blocking her throat burst. Air rushed in.

"Let's get you off the street," Gavran's voice said in her ear.

She couldn't make her eyes focus. Couldn't convince her limbs to respond even to free herself of his touch. She'd endured this year, given up her family, and where had it gotten her? Even her sacrifice was worthless.

Maybe her dadaidh was right about her after all. He'd always said she wasn't worth the food he fed her. That she couldn't do anything right. Maybe she shouldn't have bothered to try.

Or maybe she should have taken the fairy's wishes for herself and wished for her brother to be well, regardless of the consequences to Gavran. If she hadn't loved Gavran so much—If she hadn't loved Morna and Ros and Davina and Allen all so much—

Gavran let her go, and she found herself sitting on a patch of springy grass at the edge of town. She curled her arms around her knees and rocked back and forth.

Not only had her sacrifice been for nothing, but now she had to live with the knowledge that she'd made things worse for two of the people she loved. She couldn't bear it. Her life had only been tolerable before because she'd believed they were better off.

The time had come to end this.

Gavran sat silently beside her, on her right, leaning back on his hands, eyes closed. His *sgian* created a slight bulge from the underarm pocket on his left side. It'd be so easy to take it. With him nearby, she could kill herself successfully. All she had to do was slip far enough away that he wouldn't catch her in time to stop her, while staying near enough to keep the wishes at bay.

It was her only remaining choice.

CEANA RESTED A HAND ON HIS SHOULDER AND PUSHED HERSELF up, her skirts brushing against his side. He opened his eyes.

She stared down at him with dry, empty eyes. "I need a moment's privacy."

He'd expected she'd want to grieve alone once the initial shock had passed. "I'll wait here for you. Don't go far."

She walked back into the outskirts of Dunvegan and turned down between a row of houses. He didn't close his eyes again. He didn't need to now. Watching her crumble, he'd felt like someone cracked all his ribs. He couldn't draw a full breath without an unbearable ache.

Yet he could do nothing for her. His family wouldn't believe she wasn't a witch, and nothing he could say or do would change that. Once his mamaidh's mind was made up, she didn't change it, and he'd only made it worse by stealing Ceana from his dadaidh and Tavish. Brighde...he didn't even want to think what Brighde and Tavish would do.

Even if he tried to hide Ceana near him to cancel out the wishes, he couldn't keep her with him when he needed to take the sheep out to pasture or travel to town. Or when he and Brighde went to visit her family. Assuming Tavish didn't call off the betrothal because of what had already happened.

A course racket of laughter billowed from two streets over, and a pig squealed. It wasn't safe to rest here too long after dark. He touched the pocket sheath where his *sgian* should have been. It was empty.

Ceana's words from the day before about how many times she'd tried to kill herself came back to him, and heat flooded his head, sending a tingling sensation across his scalp and down into his fingers. She knew there was no going back to his home as well as he did.

He sprinted towards where she'd disappeared.

A glow from the window of one of the homes gave enough light for him to make out her figure, back turned to him, shoulders stooped. He barreled into her from the side, knocking her off balance. His *sgian* flew from her hand.

She dove after it, fingers groping in the dark. He yanked her back, and she turned on him. Her fist slammed into his cheek, and pain vibrated through his jaw, ten toothaches in a second's time.

He lost his grip on her and cupped his face with one hand. She'd actually hit him.

She lunged for the *sgian* again. He tackled her and pinned her face-down. She writhed under him, but he trapped both her arms to the ground and used his body weight to hold her in place.

If his mamaidh could see him now, rough-handling a woman, she'd box his ears no matter his age. "Did you injure yourself?"

She bucked beneath him again, weaker this time. He held on.

She stilled. He'd expected her to yell at him, but she didn't speak at all.

He lifted his weight enough to flip her over. He ran his hands over her stomach. They came away damp and sticky, but he couldn't see if it was blood. He brought his hand up to his face and gagged. Not blood. At least not blood alone.

He shifted back onto her hips and glanced over his shoulder. He had to hope no one passed by and spotted them. His intentions could easily be mistaken for something else.

He pulled up one of her sleeves. No cuts. The other arm was clean as well.

His muscles relaxed. He'd found her in time. "If it was your time to die, the Almighty would have called you home."

He slid off of her and grabbed the *sgian*.

She rolled to her side but made no move to get out of the

filth beneath her. "You have no idea what it's like. You couldn't imagine it if you tried."

He took a step back. He didn't, and he couldn't.

She was right. It took despair beyond his understanding to prefer to die in a puddle of excrement over facing another day. He couldn't even imagine it because he'd been shielded from every unhappiness and failure by the wishes she'd given up for him.

He'd thought his dreams were nightmares, but they weren't. She was the one who'd gotten the nightmare, and his entire past was a fantasy she'd created. He didn't know anything about life outside of it. What he and his family had wasn't right or natural. It wasn't what the Almighty intended for them.

He didn't even know anything about himself. The Holy Scriptures said it was in suffering that a man developed perseverance and an upright character. He'd never had to develop character or perseverance or any of the other qualities that could only be tested and known through hardship.

He knelt beside her. If this was his first true test, it'd surely be a failure if he let her kill herself. The only reason to do that was to keep the wishes for himself. In doing so, he'd show himself to be made of everything he'd feared lurked inside—selfishness and cowardice and greed.

He held up the *sgian*. "There has to be a better solution than this."

"We both know I can't go home with you."

He did know. He'd already considered and dismissed that option.

"Please, let me die." She looked up at him with eyes filled with grief also beyond his comprehension. "I can't do this anymore."

He couldn't put down a human the way he did an animal, but he couldn't expect her to continue on as she had, either. That left one solution. When a wolf discovered their sheep, and the barriers they constructed against it failed, they hunted down the wolf and killed it. "We can find the fairy and make her take back the wishes."

Something sparked in her eyes—hope? Whatever it was, she doused it as quickly as it appeared. She sat up. "You'll snatch that offer back as soon as you think through the consequences."

Whatever they'd been to each other before, Ceana Campbell didn't think very highly of him now. He tried to pull up a memory of Brighde's adoring smile to replace the discomfort in his chest Ceana's glare left behind, but the way Brighde looked at him didn't give him the same walk-on-water feeling it had before.

Maybe it wouldn't again until he could prove to himself he was the kind of man who deserved such admiration. First he had to convince Ceana that he understood the ramifications of his offer.

He'd survived life without the wishes once, as had his family.

Maybe he could win her over by showing her as much. "What was our life like before the wishes?"

"I don't know what you want me to say." She raised her shoulders up to her ears, held them there for a second, then flopped them down. "It'd be like explaining snow to someone who's never seen it. You don't even know what daily sorrows can be like. It's better for everyone, including your family, if we end this now."

"It's not better for you."

"I don't matter."

Those words sounded eerily familiar as well, an echo of something in his dream.

The urge to shelter her face in his hand and tell her she did matter hit him out of nowhere. It was as if the part of him that remembered her fought back against the part that couldn't.

She wedged her back against the wood-slatted wall of a light-less house, knees curled in to her chest and chin resting on her knees. The same way she'd sat in his dream after taking the curse of the wishes on herself and giving him the best. Giving him every joy that could have been hers.

He couldn't remember his real past, and she was right about his present, but he could remember the dream about what had happened that night. "When you used your wishes to bless me, I argued with you—begged you to take back what you'd done while the fairy would still allow it. I wouldn't have done that had

I not been prepared to continue my life as a normal man. I knew what I was doing then."

She sucked in a breath, and for a second he thought she might burst into tears—or spit in his face. "You knew exactly what you were doing. You took the wishes and left me to face the consequences."

He hadn't exactly had a choice. They hadn't been able to stop the fairy at the time, and that had left her to suffer under the curse-side. That didn't mean they couldn't do something about it now.

She'd put him before herself for long enough. It was his turn to take care of her—to care about her life when she wasn't able to.

The problem was that no argument he made based on saving her was likely to change her mind because she placed no value on her life, especially since she thought saving herself would mean harming his family. There seemed to be only one person she might be willing to find and fight this fairy for.

"It's not better for your brother, either."

Her eyes fluttered closed, and her chest rose and fell with lurching movements.

"If we rid you of the curse, you could find him and care for him." He moved a step closer. "You can still do right by him."

She opened her eyes again. They seemed to glow around the edges. "I'll do it."

CHAPTER 8

Ceana let Gavran lead her from the alleyway. Believing him might make her the biggest *eejit* to walk the moors. He'd promised her once before, right after the fairy forced the wishes on them, that he'd help her find a way out. He'd broken his promise when it mattered the most, just like her dadaidh broke promise after promise to her mamaidh, breaking her spirit in the process.

She wanted to believe this time would be different. That Gavran was the man he seemed to be in their daily life rather than who he seemed to be when he let her down in her moment of need. She needed to believe it. For the sake of her brother. She couldn't help him alone.

But this time, she'd be watchful as well in case Gavran tried to betray his promise again.

Gavran jabbed his thumb towards the edge of town. "We need to find someplace safe to sleep."

She tested out a smile. It felt foreign to her lips. "I guess that means we don't have money to stay at an inn."

"No money. No food. No blankets."

She almost laughed. No money, food, or blankets described most of her last year of life. She was used to it, but he wasn't. She wasn't going to let herself hope yet. One night on the hard ground might be what it took to show him how cruel life could be without the wishes to protect him.

"Here's our real problem," he said. "How do we catch a fairy?"

Should she find that humorous or idiotic? "Do you expect me to know because I was the one the fairy targeted?"

Gavran's shoulders hunched.

She pressed her lips together and gave a silent snort. He had thought it. He had no concept of life when you weren't fated to succeed at everything you tried. He thought the solution to this would drop at their feet and he'd be home by week's end.

They passed the outlying buildings, leaving Dunvegan behind.

He seemed to do a mental pick-up and dust-off. The hound-dog droopiness in his face vanished. "Then what we need to figure out is who would know the most about fairies. We can't succeed in this without aid."

True enough. If they were going to find the fairy and make her take back the wishes, they'd need an ally who knew more about the fae than they did. He was sure to balk at her suggestion of who to approach first, but it was the obvious choice. "We could go to a spaewife. Like as not, we'd be able to buy a cure for the curse."

Gavran coughed like he'd choked on his own tongue. "You want us to make a deal with the devil? How's that any better than being cursed by a fae?"

"We're not making a deal with the devil by speaking to a spaewife."

"She's sold her soul to him." Gavran crossed his arms over his chest. "That's close enough."

A tingle swept up the back of her neck and spread across her face. *It's the Almighty wanting to catch your attention,* her mamaidh told her when she was a little girl.

She kicked a rock. It tumbled down the dirt road in front of them. Some things were a luxury. Only people like Gavran could afford them. Her mamaidh certainly paid the price for trying to. She wasn't going to make the same mistake. She had to be practical. "Then you figure out how to learn about the fae. Anyone but the spaewife and we'll get more tall tales than fact."

The *hoo, hoo, hoo* of a male horned owl interrupted them from between the mite-blistered leaves and black, woody cones of the alder tree next to the road. From the top of the hill to their left, the raspy buzz of a female owl echoed back. The male took flight, his long ears looking like real horns in the moonlight.

Gavran rubbed his forehead right above his eyebrows, his

eye-edges crinkling the way they used to when he worked hard sums. "If all it took was buying a cure from the spaewife, why didn't you do that before?"

Ceana tilted her chin down to keep from shaking her head. The curses weren't this difficult to understand. He was an intelligent man. Maybe he was looking for an excuse to abandon her again that would also leave his conscience appeased. "I couldn't so much as find a dry place to sleep if I wanted one."

Gavran gave one brisk nod and fell silent.

Guilt nipped at the edges of her heart, and she brutally kicked it down. He deserved to feel the reality of what he'd done. Still… "And I don't know if even a spaewife will have a cure for us. But she's certain to have information on the fae."

Gavran drew in a breath that sounded like surrender. "Maybe we ought to figure out how we're going to pay first."

Why did she suddenly feel like a bully? "We'll have to steal it."

Gavran stuck an arm out in front of her and stopped her progress. "I'm sure you must have done things to survive that you wouldn't normally do, but I won't be part of that now. We have to find a way to do this that doesn't violate every right notion."

Her teeth ground together involuntarily. She'd done what she had to, and in many cases, she'd had no choice. When she wanted to do the right thing, the curse blocked her path.

Even though he acknowledged that, he'd still basically said

some lines shouldn't be crossed, no matter the circumstances. He clearly thought that even the curses didn't justify the actions she had to take. He likely had no idea how what he said made her feel, and she shouldn't have cared what he thought, but it stung in her belly, and she couldn't shake it.

He strode off again. She hesitated a second, then scrambled after him. As much as she wished to be alone for a minute, she couldn't let him get too far away. She might never find him again.

They passed into the surrounding hills.

Gavran slowed his pace. "We'll have to pick up work until we earn enough."

"Your dadaidh will find us long before we manage that."

"My dadaidh." His grin made him more handsome than he had a right to be. "That's how we'll get the money."

Aye, that sounded like a wise idea. "We'll ask your dadaidh for it," she said deadpan. "Did I hit you too hard in the head back in the alley?"

He cocked an eyebrow at her as if to ask *Are you an eejit?* "We'll take the money from my dadaidh. We won't ask him for it."

"I thought you said you wouldn't steal."

"It's not the same. We have what we do in part because of you. So we owe you what he's carrying with him."

Hearing her sacrifice acknowledged and valued, some of the

tightness in her chest bubbled away. "How do we find them? Would they have traveled home?"

"Aye. Home thinking you'd gone back for me." Gavran scratched the side of his nose for a second. "But when they found I'd gone in the night, they're wise enough to figure I'm the one who set you free. They'll have headed back to Dunvegan without resting. I'm certain Tavish will have sent one of his sons to our croft to fill my dadaidh's absence, so they'll hunt for us as long as it takes. My dadaidh will, at least."

Gavran's dadaidh had always been a supporter of Brigdhe's infatuation of Gavran because of Tavish's many sons. Linking the families meant more male hands in time of crisis. Before the wishes, Gavran had been his only boy, and even now, Finn was years from working alongside them. The wishes had given Gavran the woman who would best help his family. "So where would they camp?"

"In the same spot my dadaidh and I bed down when we come to town for market, I suspect."

"Then we should go now. We'll have to do it while they sleep."

Gavran changed directions. The moon was almost directly overhead by the time he pressed a finger to his lips and pointed in front of them. They crouched down and crept forward. Gavran dropped to his belly behind a thick patch of blackthorn bushes, and she mimicked him.

She pushed a clump of blackthorn leaves with their tiny

white flowers out of her way to get a better look at the clearing. Only one man sat by the fire, his back propped against a wagon wheel and his head tilted back. The fire at his feet smoldered with coals that had only an hour or so left on their life. They must have decided to set a watch in case she came back to curse them in their sleep, and the one who took the first watch dozed off.

She raised her eyebrows at Gavran as a question. He shrugged and leaned forward. His lips touched her ear. Her stomach betrayed her, sending flutters up into her chest. She wanted to shove him away, but forced herself to stay still.

"Looks like Tavish." His breath was warm and moist against her skin. Even with his lips touching her, she strained to hear him. "Dadaidh must be asleep in the wagon."

He pointed at the birch tree above them, at her, and then at his eyes. She shook her head emphatically and pointed from him to the tree. Even if she hadn't been able to succeed because of the wishes, she had more experience trying to nab items that didn't belong to her than he did. He should be the lookout.

His jaw tensed, and he shook his head as well.

This was foolish. She wasn't going to waste time arguing a plan with him in hand movements. Either of the men could wake and have trouble falling back asleep, and then they'd be stuck waiting for the next night, increasing their chances of being caught and separated in the meantime.

She rolled out from under the bushes and slithered forward

on her belly. She cleared the underbrush, bounced to a standing position, and edged forward, staying out of the wavering circle of light cast by the coals. For what little it mattered. With a full moon out, she might as well be standing in a clearing lit by torches.

A branch snapped behind her, and she froze. She slowly turned her head. Gavran crouched at the tree line. His expression was darker than tar, and she knew what he'd love to do if he had the feathers. He put his hands out palms up, a plea for her to stop or return—she wasn't sure which.

She held position. He patted his hip where a money pouch would hang and then held his hands up in a shrug.

She cringed. She didn't know where his dadaidh might hide his money pouch while traveling.

She waved Gavran towards her. He frowned but left the cover of the bushes. She tiptoed forward and peeked over the side of the wagon. Gavran's dadaidh lay on his back, his mouth hanging open, a soft snore vibrating from his chest. A large, gray woolen blanket covered him from chin to toes. No money pouch in sight.

Gavran stopped beside her. He pointed into the wagon and tapped his chest between his collar bones. She squished her eyes shut for a second. If his dadaidh normally kept his money pouch beneath his leine, as soon as he felt someone reaching under his blanket, he'd be up and waking Tavish, and she was no match for a man.

Gavran skewered her with a this-would-have-been-easier-under-the-bushes-where-we-could-talk look. She pretended she hadn't seen it.

She poked a finger in the direction of Tavish and mimed hitting him in the head. Gavran shook his head so hard she feared it'd topple from his neck. She nodded just as vehemently.

Course, if one of them was going to hold down Gavran's dadaidh, it ought to be Gavran. He was stronger. She picked her way to the tree line and found a heavy branch on the ground. She scooped it up and brought it back.

Gavran had planted his feet wide and folded his arms over his chest, his body language screaming that he wouldn't budge.

She pointed up into the wagon again and then put her hand over her mouth. Hopefully Gavran would figure out she wanted him to climb up and keep hold on his dadaidh while she knocked out Tavish. And hopefully he'd comply once he realized she intended to go forward with or without him.

If not, she might end up going to the kirk to stand trial for witchcraft *and* thievery.

She slipped around the tongue of the wagon and raised the branch. Tavish jerked awake and hollered.

There was the sound of a thump—Gavran launching into the wagon?—from her left. She swung her branch at Tavish, but he easily deflected it. She sprinted for the tree line. If he chased her, they might yet have a chance.

Heavy footfalls raced after her. She dodged to the left. She couldn't leave the clearing or risk going too far from Gavran. Tavish would catch her for sure if that happened.

Scuffling and thumping were definitely coming from the wagon now. She spun around and jabbed her branch back toward Tavish. He rammed into it stomach-first. He let out an *oomph*, and they rebounded in opposite directions.

The branch flew from her hands, and she hit the ground hard. She gasped for air that wouldn't come and skittered backward like a crab. Her lungs released, and she sucked in a deep breath.

Gavran launched out of the wagon, and his gaze raked the clearing. She crawled to her feet, using a tree trunk for support.

She knew the second he caught sight of her because he raced straight for her. His dadaidh climbed from the wagon, shouting.

"Go!" Gavran yelled.

He snatched her hand on the way past and dragged her along behind him.

They ran until she stumbled to her knees. Her lungs burned, and her head felt fuzzy. It'd been a long time since she'd run so far.

Gavran glanced back the way they'd come. "I think we made it, but we need to get under cover for the night. Can you stand?"

She couldn't grab enough air to answer. Gavran reached out as if he wanted to rub her back, and then pulled back. His hands were empty. Where was the money pouch? They wouldn't get a second chance.

"Did we...get...the...money?" Each word was a struggle.

He patted his belt. "I got it. But they'll be hunting for us harder and longer now. Like as not they think you've bewitched me into becoming a criminal. They'll want to rescue me before you get me hung."

She forced her legs to straighten. "Let's find somewhere safe to hide for the night. We can visit the spaewife to buy the cure on the morrow. Then you can go home and tell them that's exactly what I did."

CHAPTER 9

Gavran lengthened his strides to catch Ceana, and they melded into the mid-morning market crowd milling on the outskirts of Dunvegan. Hopefully the noise would at last drown out the memories of his dadaidh's accusations from the night before. Even though he should have slept dreamless, he couldn't, kept awake by the remembrance of the betrayed look in his dadaidh's eyes and the sounds of him desperately trying to convince Gavran that this wasn't him and that *the witch* controlled him.

He pulled Ceana to a stop in front of a stall selling bannocks. He paid for three and handed two to her.

When he'd suggested taking the money from his dadaidh, he hadn't counted on how his mind wouldn't be able to rest afterward. He kept trying to come up with a way they could have done it differently and how he might make amends.

Almost worse, he didn't know what to call what was happening, and it itched in his brain. He couldn't even tell Ceana about it and ask her because she'd warned him. If he asked her, she'd think he meant to back out.

All he could do was make sure the money helped pay Ceana back for what she'd sacrificed.

And pray Ceana spoke true that seeking help from a spaewife wasn't sinning against the Almighty. It seemed every right he tried to do forced him into a choice between two wrongs.

"Where do we find this spaewife?" he asked.

Ceana took a big enough bite of her first cake that oats stuck to her top lip. She licked them away. "Spaewives usually pitch their tent on the busiest side of the market, offering to tell fortunes." Her words were garbled by the mouthful of food. "My mamaidh—"

Her voice caught and she coughed. She cleared her throat. "My mamaidh never let us have our future read, said only the Almighty could know what was to come. But she'd often buy one o' her remedies for keeping away the fae 'cause even the brownies couldn't be trusted. They were too easy to offend, and then you'd find your house worse off than before."

Gavran finished his bannock and wiped his hand on his trews. His mamaidh said the same. Some of the fae were generous in their help to common folk, but beware of offending them. It was better to care for your own than to take a favor from a fae.

They moved away from the bannock seller, and Ceana dipped down, out of his peripheral vision. He turned back.

She knelt on one knee in front of a boy so scrawny that his age was near impossible to guess. He sat cross-legged on the packed ground and stared off center of where he should, his eyes cloudy.

Pressure bloomed in Gavran's chest. This feeling was new and strange as well—a heaviness unconnected to a physical injury.

Ceana picked up the boy's hand and placed her second bannock in it. She whispered something to him and rose to her feet.

She took a quick stride as if she'd expected to have to chase after Gavran and stuttered to a stop. Pink flushed her cheeks. "He needed the bannock more than meself. I'd see him there whenever I was in town. I couldn't help him before, and I always swore I would if I could."

She made it sound as if the boy regularly begged in this spot, but in all his visits to the market, Gavran couldn't remember seeing him once. "He's always there?"

Ceana nodded and wove her way through the market day crowd.

"You're certain?" Gavran fell into step beside her. "I haven't noticed him before this day."

Ceana's eyes narrowed, then her face smoothed. Her mouth twitched. "'Course not."

She craned her neck from left to right as if searching for the spaewife's tent or keeping watch.

He ought to be watching, too, for his dadaidh and Tavish, but the boy and the feeling in his chest ground away at him. What kind of a selfish clot was he not to notice a starving blind child?

Though, Ceana wasn't glaring at him accusingly, and she certainly had no trouble telling him of his other failings. "Why wouldn't I have seen him?"

"You're living outside the wishes now." She stopped, and the crowd flowed around them, brushing and bumping as they passed. "You didn't see him when you walked with the blessings because it would have saddened you."

The feeling was sadness. She said it so matter-of-factly, but to never have experienced sadness…Maybe he should be thankful for that. This feeling wasn't one he'd wish on another. But to not experience it meant he either felt no sympathy for others or, like with the boy, didn't see their suffering at all.

His mouth turned to old leather inside. He couldn't begin to wrap his mind around what he'd never experienced thanks to Ceana's wishes. They'd spared him, but they'd also cut short his ability to do any real good in the world, for he couldn't see the depth of suffering happening around him.

"There she is," Ceana said.

She pointed towards a double-belled wedge tent pitched on the fringes. The tent was the kind used more often on the northern reaches of the isle by those whose tent was also their home. The wedge shape and triangular cross-section would give her the maximum amount of space inside while still being able to withstand the worst nature lobbed at her.

The tent flap was down.

"Do we knock?" he asked.

Ceana rapped on the fabric, and the front of the tent rippled.

A woman his mamaidh's age with dark hair and skin pale as curdled cream opened the flap for them. Somehow he'd expected her to be old and haggard.

"We need to hire your services," Ceana said.

Without a word, the woman stepped aside and held the flap open for them.

Directly in front of them stood a table no bigger than a barrel top, with two rickety chairs Gavran doubted would hold his weight. Along the shorter side of the tent to the right lay the woman's narrow bed, covered in red and brown blankets. Smoke from a fire foolishly lit inside made the room as hot as the type of summer day where you didn't even have the energy to swat flies. The smell of lavender, thyme, spearmint, and smoke filled his throat to bursting and burned his eyes.

The spaewife motioned at the chairs. "You're here to buy, not to have the future told."

Gavran's skin crawled. She might have guessed their purpose, but there was no way she could have known.

"So what is it then that you be needing?" the spaewife asked.

Ceana ignored the offered chair, but shuffled a little closer, the money sack in her hand. "A cure. For a fae curse."

"Cures for fae curses are complicated." The spaewife held out her hand, palm up, and rubbed her thumb, pointer, and middle fingers together. "They come with a steep price. Let me see what you have, and whether it'll be enough."

Ceana handed over the money sack.

The spaewife poured the coins into her hand and poked through them with a finger. The coins caught the light from the flames as if they would catch fire as well.

The spaewife dumped the coins into a trunk at the back of the tent, locked the lid, and handed the empty purse back to Ceana. "I usually ask for more, but I'll make an exception."

Gavran couldn't keep his hand from moving to cover his own hidden coin purse. Surely she would have said the same no matter how much they offered her. Ceana had wanted to give the spaewife everything in the money sack, but he'd taken out a few coins. Once the spaewife cured the curse, he'd be able to go home or find his dadaidh and claim he convinced Ceana to release her hold on him, but she'd have nothing and no one to turn to. He needed to be sure she could at least eat until she found honest work.

The spaewife circled the tent pole, touching one bundle of herbs hanging from it, then the next. The spiky needles of rosemary, the white flowers of chamomile, and many others even his mamaidh likely wouldn't recognize.

The spaewife stopped and broke a stalk free, moved on and plucked another. She tossed them into the pot of boiling liquid over the fire. "Fae curses are unique to the type of fae who cursed you and to what they wanted you to suffer from. I'll need more information to finish the potion. Was it a trow?"

Ceana glanced back at Gavran.

He shrugged. He had no idea how to tell one fae from another. He'd never seen one outside of his dream—or the night the dream happened.

Ceana ran her tongue over the edge of her lips. "I don't believe so. We thought she was a fairy. She looked like a woman. Tall, slender. Hair the same color as mine. But she seemed...I felt as though I could see through her even though she was solid."

The spaewife pulled a jar from a shelf and flicked a pinch of seeds into the liquid. "And the curse itself?"

"I cannot succeed at anything I try, and I'll never find love or happiness."

The spaewife's glanced at Gavran, but her expression remained passive. "Is that all?"

He brushed a hand over his face. The smoke built a barrier in his throat that he couldn't clear. Even though her expression hadn't changed when she'd shifted her gaze to him, he'd have sworn it carried an accusation. Or perhaps that was only his own conscience projecting his own emotions outward.

Ceana gave a tiny shake of her head. "I never dream of the

night we met her, and he receives the opposite of everything I'm cursed with."

The spaewife picked up a bottle this time. The glass was thick and green, but the liquid that oozed from the dipper was red like blood.

The spaewife ladled out a scoop from the pot into another glass bottle. "You must not drink this within the town. There's too much iron here, too many things that dilute the power of fae and cures for the ills they cause."

Ceana's hands trembled.

Gavran stepped forward and accepted the bottle from the spaewife. If she dropped it, they couldn't afford another. He tucked it inside his cloak.

He ushered Ceana from the tent. Her tremors shook the hand he rested on her back.

As soon as they were out of the tent, she reached for his pocket. "Let me see it."

He brushed her hands away. "You heard what she said. Not here."

"I won't drink it. I just want to hold it."

He wouldn't let her impulsiveness win this time. Look where that'd gotten them last night. "It could get knocked from your hand or stolen by a beggar who thinks they can sell it for a few pennies."

She scowled at him and stalked ahead toward the edge of the market.

He caught the sound of his dadaidh's voice through the murmur of the crowd and yanked Ceana back, behind a cart.

The look she shot him was full of confusion. "What are you doing?"

He peered around the cart. His dadaidh was only two stalls away, talking to a fishmonger. Ceana pushed close.

He nudged her backwards. "My dadaidh's near enough to see us if we kept going that way."

She ground her knuckles into her skirt. "Is Tavish with him?"

"I couldn't tell. Might be they've come to see the spaewife themselves." He winked at her. "And find out how to stop a witch."

Ceana clamped both hands over her mouth, but a laugh spilled from between her fingers anyway. Her eyes crinkled at the corners.

Her laugh was more beautiful than church bells, light and rich and giving him a sense of peace in the center of his soul. Once the curse was gone, some man would hear it, and she'd have someone to care for her the way she deserved.

The thought felt vaguely familiar again. A muscle pulsed in his cheek. It was like being caught in cobwebs that he couldn't wipe off to not know what he'd said in the past to Ceana, what things had been like between them before.

She stiffened, and a grey sheet fell over her face. "She'll know they mean us if they describe what we look like. You don't think she'll tell your dadaidh we were there, do you?"

The carnivorous look in the spaewife's eyes as she counted out their coins with her finger lay fresh in his mind. Whether she turned on them or not depended on how much Tavish and his dadaidh offered.

He cocked his head towards a gap between two tents. "No sense waiting to find out."

She led the way, and he followed. He had to shuffle along sideways to fit through the narrow passage. They came out the other side and cut over two rows of houses.

He let out the breath he'd been holding. Before nightfall, this would all be over.

They walked until they couldn't see Dunvegan, because every time he suggested they were far enough away, Ceana wanted to keep going. To make sure they were truly far enough from town for the potion to work.

The vial in his pocket grew heavier with each step, almost as if it didn't want to be drunk. That was likely his own fleshly self again, having second thoughts he shouldn't have and attributing them to an object that couldn't think or feel.

"Where are you going?" Ceana called.

He stopped. She wasn't in front of him anymore. He spun around.

She waited under a blossoming apple tree. "I think we're far enough now. Give me the vial."

He trekked back to her and pulled it from his pocket. Once she drank it, there was no turning back. The wishes would be gone. His family would be on their own. The way he'd felt today would be the norm.

Perhaps she'd been right, and he'd regret giving up the protection of the wishes.

Ceana snatched the bottle from his hand, popped the cork with her thumb, and chugged the liquid.

Her eyes were hard as flint stone. "You were going to back out. I could see it."

"I wasn't." His voice kicked up to a higher pitch. He wasn't sure what he'd been about to do.

Ceana wriggled the cork back into the empty bottle. "You haven't changed that much. It was the same look you had when you were going to let me drown. You're good at making promises and terrible at keeping them."

He barely stopped himself from grabbing her and shaking her. It wasn't so much that she drank the potion. It was that she hadn't given him a chance to decide. Just like she hadn't given him a chance on the night of the wishes. How was he supposed to prove to her, to himself, that he could be a man of honor if she never gave him the chance? "You don't know that."

She laughed. Not the beautiful sound of before but harsh and brittle and much too old.

"I think I know you better than you know yourself." She tucked the bottle away. "But it doesn't matter now. This time I was prepared. I did what it took to protect myself. And I'd do it again."

All spirit of camaraderie he'd thought he'd felt growing between them sizzled out. He nodded once, businesslike. "Let's figure out if this worked. It's clear enough you'll be happier once we can go our separate ways."

"How do we figure out if it worked?" Her voice lost both its edge and its age. A lost little girl stood in front of him where a bitter old woman had been seconds before. "We can't test it unless we're apart, but if it hasn't worked, I won't be able to find you again."

After she'd near enough called him an untrustworthy lout, she still expected him to stick around if this didn't work.

And he would. Because doing anything else would prove her right.

He shook his head. "I'm sure it worked. You said yourself your mamaidh bought potions from the spaewives. She must have trusted their skills."

He might as well have drowned a bag full of kittens for the look she gave him.

He rubbed his eyes. They still felt gritty from lack of sleep and the spaewife's smoky tent. Even if he had to live without the wishes after this, at least he'd get some sleep. "The wishes work by making you fail?"

"Aye."

"So pick something simple." He scooped up a handful of apple blossom petals from the ground beneath the tree. "Decide you want to fill your pockets with these."

She crouched down and ran her fingertips through the petals. "But you'll have to come back to me. To check. If it didn't work—"

"I know. You won't be able to find me." He let the blossoms fall from his hands. "I'll return before sunset."

CEANA SETTLED IN UNDER THE TREE. SHE WASN'T SURE HOW FAR away he needed to be. She counted to three hundred and reached out a hand.

She hesitated with her fingers hovering over the pile of petals. It must have worked. Everyone went to the spaewives for magical cures. Gossip even said they sold a few curses to feuding neighbors, so they must know how to cure them if they could create them.

She closed her hand around the glossy petals and tucked the first fist-full into the empty money pouch at her waist. She continued until it was near to bursting.

Pouch full, she slouched back against the tree and counted to twenty. If she was cured, when she reached her hand in again, the petals should still be there.

She slid her hand inside the pouch and her skin brushed the same silky softness. She pulled out a handful and blew them off her palm. They twisted and fluttered in the air for a second like they might take flight before floating to the ground.

She felt light enough to fly with them, so buoyant her weight shouldn't have been enough to keep her earthbound.

At last. She was free.

She swirled her fingers through the rest of the petals, pulled the pouch up to her face, and breathed in the sweet fragrance.

She scooped up another handful and shoved it in. And another and another.

What would it be like to live free from the curse of the wishes? What could she do with her life?

Though what she did mattered less than that she could do something. She could find her brother, and somehow she'd earn enough to feed them. She'd survived having nothing, so even if they had very little, it'd feel like a wealth of riches. More importantly, they'd be together again, and she could keep him safe.

She let her eyes drift shut and tilted her face up to catch the warmth of the sun. Drowsiness settled over her.

Someone gently shook her, and her eyes opened sluggishly. A man stood over her, his face too dark to see because of the sun at his back. She shaded her eyes, and Gavran's features became clear. Of course it was Gavran. In her fear, she'd made him promise to come back to check on her.

She flashed him a smile. "It worked."

His return smile was hollow as a robbed grave, but she'd expected no less. He'd offered to give up the wishes, but now he had to face the consequences of that action.

"It worked?" he asked.

She unbundled her cloak. She'd show him the petals to prove it.

She sank her hand into her pouch.

It was empty.

Her heart seemed to tick to a stop. Or maybe time slowed and her heart beat in synch to the new tempo.

It had to be the wrong pouch. She still had the one Davina lent her along with the clothes. Maybe she'd filled that one, only thinking she'd tucked the petals into the larger coin pouch.

She reached into the second pouch.

Empty.

CEANA'S FACE WENT FROM THE ANGELIC PINK FLUSH OF SLEEP TO pale as a three-day old corpse. Her lips faded away, and her eyes widened, her gaze flicking.

He knelt beside her. "What's wrong?"

She turned out his dadaidh's coin pouch. "They're not there. They were there, and now they're not."

Gavran bit back a curse. As he'd walked the moors, he'd convinced himself he was glad to be done with it and be able to return home even though he'd lost the blessing of the wishes.

Now they weren't done at all. The fairy who cursed Ceana seemed to have created the wishes to give them enough tether to run ahead and think they were free, only to be jerked back.

"You must have put them in before I was out of the boundary, and they disappeared once I was."

"It's hopeless then." Ceana tightened and loosened the string on the coin purse. "I'll be bound forever."

They wouldn't solve this problem if she focused on the dark side of things every time they encountered an obstacle. "We've only tried once. You give up too easily."

She yanked the string, and it made a snapping sound. "As would you if you'd spent even a season where everything you tried could only fail."

"You can't blame the wishes. In my dream, you wanted to give up and drown."

"And you would have let me."

He felt the words like another jab to his face. He didn't know what he would have done had the fairy not snatched them from the water. In the dream, he had considered letting her drown to save himself. It'd been a fleeting thought, but it'd been there nonetheless.

Perhaps it was that selfish cowardice, and not that he'd ended up blessed by the wishes instead of her, that made her hate him now. "Why did you give me the best of the wishes, then? If I'm so despicable?"

"I didn't do it for you. I did it for my brother. I thought if I was erased, he would be whole."

She chewed the edge of her lip and dropped her gaze to the coin purse.

He didn't know how he knew, but he knew it meant she was lying. He took the balled-up coin purse from her hands and tucked it into his belt. "You could have kept the wishes for yourself and been more sure of helping your brother."

She squeezed her eyes shut, ashamed to face him or blocking the path of unwanted tears, he wasn't sure which. "You were family to me, too. You looked out for me better than my own family ever did. You were only out in the loch that night because of me."

Resolving the break between them felt like digging broken pieces of glass from beach sand and trying to mend them back together. They were worn so smooth that maybe it was impossible.

But if either of them was to have any peace—if they were going to be able to work together to solve this—he had to try. Their common enemy was too powerful for them to continue fighting each other as well. "Will you tell me what happened that night? I assumed our boat overturned. The dream always starts with us in the water."

"I wish it were as simple as an overturned boat. Then it would have been an accident and not something I caused." Ceana pulled the spaewife's bottle from her pocket and clenched it in her hands. She turned it around and around so the glass sometimes caught the fading sun and other times looked as opaque as obsidian. "I was out on the loch sandbar digging for cockles because my dadaidh drank himself unconscious, again, instead of collecting what we'd need to sell." She looked off over his shoulder. "You came looking for me and offered to help, but I wouldn't let you. I wanted to prove to my dadaidh I could help him same as the son he thought I'd stole from him. That night was my last chance. He planned to promise me to a widower with five sons the next day."

Fury blazed in his belly until he started to believe he might be able to breathe fire. If he knew where Ceana's dadaidh was, he'd flog him until he never wanted to see another bottle of mead again.

His betrothal to Brighde would help secure the help of Tavish's sons during planting and harvest, but it'd been done with his agreement. Even though Morna and Ros were girls, his dadaidh would never trade them away or make plans for their future without their consent. "He was bartering you?"

"In a way. Robbie, the widower, promised he'd send over the two middle boys to live with my dadaidh and help him." She heaved the bottle hard. It arched through the air and rattled down through a tree. "If I could go back and do it over, I'd never have gone out to the loch that night. I'd have married Robbie Forsyth. At least then my brother would be safe and I wouldn't be stuck like this."

Robbie Forsyth. He knew the man. Robbie worshipped his first wife, and that should have meant he'd treat the one he wed last summer the same way. But all anyone heard from him was how much better his first wife had been at everything—from the cooking to the mending to the marital relations. His second wife's empty eyes haunted Gavran every time he saw her. She deserved better. And so did Ceana. "You don't mean that."

She tilted her head to the side and just stared at him.

His chest constricted. She did mean it.

He took a risk and cupped her cheek in his palm, an image of her giving her bannock to the boy playing in his mind. "Then it'd be a shame. I'd hate to see you trade yourself for a fraction of what you're worth." He nodded towards Dunvegan. "Let's go back and find out from the spaewife why the potion didn't work."

CHAPTER 10

G avran's dadaidh turned back in her direction, and Ceana ducked down behind the wagon she and Gavran were using as cover.

There was no way they'd be able to go in the front of the spaewife's tent. The spaewife must have told Allan and Tavish that they'd been to see her because now the two men and three others, including a priest, loitered near her tent, trying to look casual but not-so-surreptitiously watching the crowd in the hope she and Gavran would return.

And they had.

She rubbed her temples. What must it be like to have a dadaidh who loved you that much, enough to not give up on you even after you'd attacked him and stolen his money? She pushed the thought away. Comparing her family to Gavran's wouldn't do any good. It never had.

Gavran rocked back on his heels, away from the edge of the cart. "We'll need to go in the back of the tent."

"How?"

He pulled his *sgian* from its hidden pocket. "I'll slice the fabric, and we'll have to catch her before she screams."

Not the best plan, but she couldn't come up with anything better.

Gavran squatted into a runner's stance. He shot across the opening between the cart and the spaewife's tent. As soon as the tent shielded him from sight again, he turned and nodded to her.

Ceana peeped through the wheel spokes one last time. With Gavran nearby, she had as good a chance as anyone of making it across without being spotted. The crowd was thick since they'd chosen the busiest time of the day to return to the market, and the ox harnessed to the cart stood between her and the men looking for them.

The men all seemed to be facing away. She skittered across next to Gavran. He caught her, stopping her momentum before she crashed into the tent in her haste.

"I'll make the cut," Gavran whispered. "You duck inside and grab her."

Ceana tried to ignore the thumping of her heart in her chest, but it was like trying to ignore being trampled on by a plow horse. If they were caught now, she'd be executed as a witch for sure. No one would believe Gavran when he claimed to have acted of his own free will.

And all it would take for them to be discovered was one hint of a scream from the spaewife.

Gavran raised his *sgian,* and Ceana dipped her head. She was ready.

He slashed through the thick fabric, the ripping noise soft enough it shouldn't have been heard by the men out front above the noises of the market. She burst through the hole and crashed into the spaewife. They dropped to the ground.

Ceana clamped a hand over the woman's mouth. The spaewife stared up at her with wide eyes but, surprisingly, didn't struggle, as if she'd had the air knocked out of her.

Gavran ducked in and knelt beside them, his *sgian* still in hand. He made his fake fierce face—squinty eyes, lips parted in a snarl—that she knew so well from their play sword-fights as children.

But maybe the spaewife would believe it. Ceana wiped her face of expression in support of Gavran.

"Stay quiet and we won't hurt you," he said. "But if you let them know we're here, I'll kill you before they can stop us. Understood?"

Ceana slid off the woman and inched her hand away from the spaewife's mouth. The woman gasped for breath. She had knocked the wind out of her. She knew from experience after her tussle with Tavish that she couldn't have said two words, let alone screamed. Perhaps the Almighty looked out for them after all.

The spaewife sat up and dragged herself back. She wedged herself against a table leg. "What do you want?"

"The potion you sold us didn't work. We want one that does."

The spaewife's forehead smoothed, and her eyes shrunk down from their owl-like enlargement. She drew her cloak up over her shoulders. "You're too impatient, child. Cures take time."

Ceana held out her hand to Gavran. "Give me the *sgian*."

He frowned but handed it over.

Ceana nestled it close to the woman's neck. Each time the spaewife drew a breath, her skin kissed the blade's edge. "This isn't boils or whooping cough. I know how this curse works, and if it isn't gone now, it's not going to magically clear up over time."

The spaewife's fingers tapped the hem of her cloak—one, two, three, four, three, two, one. "How did you get this curse again?"

Ceana held the *sgian* steady. "We were pulled from the water, near to drowning, by a fairy."

The spaewife lost her grip on her cloak, and it slipped off one shoulder. A sprig of heather pinned to her leine poked out from underneath the edge. A strange ornament for a woman on MacLeod lands. She should take care who saw it or she risked being accused of loyalty to the MacDonalds, the MacLeods' sworn enemies.

Without removing the *sgian* from the spaewife's neck, Ceana shifted the woman's cloak back over the heather sprig with her free hand. She knew what it was to be wrongly accused. She'd not wish that on another, even if the woman had sold them a useless potion.

The spaewife's gaze dipped a fraction, enough to tell Ceana she noticed the gesture but not enough to look directly at where the heather lay. An innocent woman would have looked straight at it.

"You have a real curse." The spaewife selected each word with the care of someone picking berries in a stinging nettle patch.

She must have interpreted Ceana's covering the heather as a bigger threat than the *sgian* at her neck. The *sgian* would kill her quick. A MacDonald spy would suffer slowly. "Of course we do. That's why we came to you to buy a cure."

The spaewife pressed her fingers to the sides of her nose. "How was I supposed to know you had a real curse on you?"

Ceana glanced at Gavran. Deep furrows scarred the space between his eyebrows.

The spaewife continued to rub the sides of her nose. "People come to me thinking they're cursed because their neighbor threatened them or they had a bad season with their crops." She shook her head like she couldn't stop herself. "A real curse is rare."

"Can you cure a real one?"

The spaewife gave a short, bark-like laugh and dropped her hands from her face. "Nae. And I'm not fool enough to meddle with the fae even if I could. Crossing them leads to worse consequences than whatever curse you might be under."

Gavran shifted beside her. She glanced at him again. He splayed and fisted his hands. For as long as she'd known him, he'd stretched out his hands that way before starting a task he dreaded. Like a fighter preparing to throw a punch at his best friend.

Her fingers went cold. Perhaps she was acting unfair to Gavran to insist he do this. But he'd promised—twice now—and shouldn't a person also be made to bear out their promises?

She turned back to the spaewife and lowered the *sgian*. "There must be something we can do about the curse."

"Go home. Try to live your lives around it as best you can. Seeking a real cure will only make your situation worse as soon as the fairy who cursed you realizes what you're up to."

"Going home isn't an option," Gavran said. "You must know of someone who can help us even if you can't."

The spaewife's glance dipped towards the hidden heather in that telltale way again.

"Few things could be worse than continuing under my curse," Ceana said. "Please. If you know who can help us, all we ask is a chance."

The spaewife set her lips in a way that said she didn't intend to budge regardless of threats or begging. "The one person who might be a help to you has had enough heartache thanks to the fae. You'd only stir up more by seeking her out. I won't allow it."

Ceana chewed the inside of her cheek. It was a stretch, but the *person* the spaewife fought so hard to protect could be Lady MacDonald. Wearing the MacDonald heather was too big a risk for loyalty to anyone lesser. All the rumors around Lady MacDonald hinted she'd angered the fae and that she never left Duntulm Castle.

She didn't even need the spaewife to admit to it. She merely needed some sign that her suspicion hit the truth. "Lady MacDonald would be the first to take pity on someone cursed by the fae."

The spaewife's body twitched. Hardly a movement.

One she wouldn't have paid any attention to had she not been digging. One she could have imagined. But it was enough, especially since they didn't have any better leads.

"Where's Duntulm Castle?" she asked Gavran.

Gavran gave her a *nicely done* smile.

His smile sent warmth racing up her limbs. It felt nice to make someone proud.

More importantly, if he'd seen the twitch, too, at least she hadn't wished it into existence. Gavran had always been more perceptive than she was when it came to people.

"It's near the northmost tip of the isle. A good two or three days by foot." Gavran parted the tent flap no wider than a finger's width. "They're still out there."

The spaewife had told them she wouldn't allow them to bring trouble to Lady MacDonald's doorstep. If they let her go, she'd sound the alarm before they could escape. The warmth in her veins turned to ice. "She'll tell them where she sent us. We have to kill her."

Gavran grabbed for his *sgian*. Ceana jerked it away.

He tugged at the end of the rope around her waist. "We can tie her up and gag her. You don't need blood on your hands."

Her hands were already so dirty no one'd even see the blood. He'd near enough said so himself. She pointed the *sgian* at his chest. "It'd be worth it. To be free of this curse."

"You say that now, but you'd regret it later. I won't let you do that to yourself."

Movement flashed in her peripheral vision. The spaewife darted for the door, screaming.

Gavran grabbed Ceana's arm, pocketed the *sgian*, and hauled her back through the rip he'd made earlier in the tent backing. Men piled through the entrance of the tent as she and Gavran fled through the back.

"Which way?" she asked.

"We need to get into the crowd. We can't move as fast, but neither can they. Maybe we can lose them."

Gavran sprinted to the left, and she took off after him. They dodged between a fishmonger's stall and a cart full of last season's withered turnips. Gavran slipped into the market-day mob.

A firm hand seized her sleeve and tugged her back.

CHAPTER 11

"Gavran!" Her throat felt like it would split apart with the strain. If he went too far away, she was doomed. "Gavran!"

She twisted, but the man holding her clinched a hand on her other arm. He wore the juniper clan badge of the MacLeods on his bonnet. What chance could they have of escape if the whole force of Dunvegan and the MacLeods hunted for them?

She kicked the man in the shin. He cursed her and corkscrewed her arm. She yelped.

His head snapped to the side, and his eyes rolled back. He collapsed. She stumbled backward.

Gavran caught her. "I've never had to hit anyone before."

There was a lot she'd never done before the curses forced her to change the way she lived. The guilt would pass. Mostly.

"There they are," the voice of Gavran's dadaidh shouted. "Stop them. They're cutpurses."

Ceana and Gavran plunged into the crowd. She glanced back. The mass of people parted behind them, giving their pursuers a clear path.

She smashed into something solid yet soft, and juggler's bags rained down around her. More curses filled the air.

Gavran dragged her past two musicians with fiddles still on their shoulders and their mouths gaping open. They wove through the yellow, black, and blue bolts of cloth at the next stall and came out of the other side of the market.

"Should we try to hide or make it out of the town?" Gavran asked.

"Out." Her shoulder throbbed from where she'd collided with the juggler. She could only pray she hadn't broken or dislocated something. "If they rally the town, all they'll have to do is wait until we need food or water."

They ducked underneath laundry hung between two huts to dry. The raisiny scent of fresh bread baking over a fire wafted from one window, and Ceana's stomach pinched. She'd been more spoiled by the good cooking of Davina Anderson than she wanted to admit.

They passed the edge of town and slipped into a cove of trees.

Ceana leaned her back against a tree trunk to catch her breath. "Do you know the way to Duntulm Castle?"

"I can get us near enough." Gavran wiped sweat from his upper lip. His sleeve left a smear visible even across the stubble. "But we can't take the open roads."

She pushed away from the tree and took off again. Hesitation meant certain defeat now that their pursuers knew where they were headed.

She didn't hear him behind her. She stopped and turned. He stared back at Dunvegan. "What are you doing?"

"My dadaidh's sure to hire at least one dog to track us. We need to figure a way to throw them off."

"Can't we just travel down a stream?"

Gavran rapped his fingers on the tree trunk. "That would throw off a man but won't stop a good dog. They're trained to follow a scent in the air, not only on the ground."

And they'd never be able to outrun them if Tavish and Allan managed to borrow horses. It was hopeless. She kicked at a pile of dead evergreen needles. "They'll still smell our scent?"

Gavran's fingers continued to absently stroke the bark. "We could disguise our scent. With fish. It wouldn't trick the dogs for long, but it might confuse them enough to give us a chance to reach Duntulm Castle."

"Even if we had a line or a spear, we'd never have the time to catch one before they caught us."

"I wasn't thinking of catching one." Gavran took her by the shoulders and maneuvered her so, in a break between the trees, she could see the main road leading from Dunvegan. A wagon bobbed along it. "I was thinking of sneaking back into Dunvegan and hiding in the cart of one of the fishmongers when they leave."

It could work. Assuming they could get back into the market without getting caught.

———

GAVRAN STOOD IN FRONT OF THE LAUNDRY LINE THEY'D PASSED on their way out, his arms crossed over his chest. It seemed they couldn't follow through on a single idea without differing on how they should go about it.

Ceana fished a woman's leine off the line. "We have to take these. Anyone who's still at the market will recognize us otherwise."

"I told you before. I won't steal from innocents."

"We'll leave our clothes in exchange. It's not stealing. It's trading."

He raised his eyebrows and glanced significantly down at his stained trews. "Our dung-covered clothes?"

"I washed them."

She had, but in the cold stream water, the stains hadn't come out, nor had all the smell.

It was one thing to take money from his father, money her wishes gave them. But he wasn't going to make someone suffer who bore no blame in their situation.

Ceana couldn't have been like this before the fairy curses. The woman in his dream was his closest friend. He'd admired her. Trusted her. Maybe even loved her.

It was hard to reconcile the woman who gave her meager food to a child with the woman willing to take clothes that didn't belong to her. It was like she had a split personality—the woman she wanted to be and the one the curses had trained her to become.

Men's voices and heavy footsteps plodded by on the street. Ceana and Gavran dove deeper into the shadows of the alley.

The voices faded away, and Gavran returned to the clothes. If they delayed much longer, the market would end, and the fishmonger's cart would be gone. He had to find a way to both take the clothes and not harm the family they belonged to.

He shoved his hands into the warmth of his cloak, and his right hand bumped his coin purse. It still held the coins he'd stashed there before they visited the spaewife. Near enough coin to replace whatever they took.

He slid out two smaller coins, just enough to buy them a bite of food along the way, and slid the larger cloak off the line.

Ceana's I-knew-you'd-see-it-my-way smile grated on him, but he didn't bother to correct her. If she remembered the coins, she'd want to keep them all. She was better off not knowing.

He turned his back on Ceana to give her privacy and donned the man's leine, trews, and short jacket. He wrapped the fresh cloak around his shoulders and fastened it with his own clasp.

"You may turn around," Ceana said softly.

He did, and his brain seemed to stutter to a stop. The deep V neckline of the dress and the white sleeves of her fresh leine that flared into a bell shape from her elbows to her wrists gave Ceana's body curves it didn't have before. The fabric's rich walnut color brought out the brown highlights in her red hair and made her brown eyes look almost golden.

She was beautiful.

She smoothed her hair, looped the striped cloak around her, and pinned it at her throat with the broach his mamaidh had lent her.

She looked so different that only his dadaidh and Tavish would recognize her. Hopefully the same held true about him.

They strolled out into the emptying market square like a couple headed home. He didn't see his dadaidh or Tavish anywhere. They were likely already out trying to hunt them down, but that didn't mean they hadn't left others in the square.

They passed the skinner's cart. The reek of burned skin and hair hung heavy in the air. As often as he visited the market, he never got used to certain smells, and one of them was that of hide fresh from tanning. If pain had a smell, he'd always imaged that would be it.

Ceana moved in as if examining a pelt. He joined her and glanced out of the corner of his eye toward the fishmonger he'd remembered. The man had already loaded up most of what hadn't sold. Had they delayed any longer over the clothes, they would have missed him. He was the only one at the market that Gavran had seen whose catch looked like he'd traveled from the north, the same direction as Duntulm Castle.

The man hefted the last barrel into the back of his cart and strode to the front. He climbed into the seat and snapped the reins across his ox's back. The cart lurched forward.

Gavran tapped Ceana's elbow. They moved off together after the cart. They needed to wait until they were out of the market's main thoroughfare where they'd be more likely to be spotted hopping in the fishmonger's cart.

The cart turned down a side street. No one was around, and the near-empty barrels bounced and rattled loudly, providing the cover they'd need.

He exchanged a glance with Ceana. She took two bouncing steps, grabbed the edge of the open cart back, and rolled inside.

He kept his distance and waited. No one called out or seemed to have noticed her nabbing a ride.

He marched forward and swung up onto the back as if the cart belonged to him and it was the most natural thing in the world for him to hop in while it was already moving. As soon as he was up, he pressed himself flat against the bottom and wiggled in between the barrels next to Ceana. Hopefully the barrels would hide them from passersby. If the driver looked back into the cart, there'd be no hiding from him.

His chest pressed into Ceana's back, and his nose buried in the top of her hair. Even with the stench of day-old fish all around them, her hair still smelled like the evergreen needles they'd slept on last night. He couldn't help himself from taking an extra breath.

Ceana stiffened, and he cringed. She must have noticed. He was an *eejit*. He hadn't meant anything by it. Assuming Tavish still allowed it, he had no choice but to wed Brighde before the next full moon. His dadaidh had given his word. A man's word needed to mean something, or what did he have left?

A weighed-down feeling ballooned in his chest until it felt like it would force his heart and lungs from his body. He recognized it this time—sadness.

Brighde must be a good woman or the wishes wouldn't have chosen her, but in the short time Ceana's presence had cancelled out the wishes, he'd noticed troubling elements of Brighde's personality. He'd no way of knowing how many more he'd discover upon returning home.

Still, Brighde loved him, and strong marriages had been built on less.

He wriggled backward to put more space between himself and Ceana, but his back hit a barrel. There was nowhere for him to go. He gave up before he accidentally rocked a barrel and drew the fishmonger's notice. He made sure his upper arm rested flat against his side, not touching Ceana.

The clatter of wagon wheels over the cobblestones of the Dunvegan roads turned to the crunch of stones and then to the soft grind of dirt. He shifted his head for a better view. He couldn't see over the side of the wagon, but trees hung over top of them now rather than chimneys and billows of smoke. At least they'd left town. Every mile they could gain from town made it less likely the dogs would pick up their trail.

He relaxed his head against the slimy bottom of the cart and let the rocking ease some of the strain that'd knotted his shoulders since he cut Ceana loose from the tree two nights ago. He allowed his eyes to drift shut.

Something warm and soft squirmed along the length of his body.

Gavran's eyes flew open. He'd dozed again. He blinked to clear his eyes of the fog of sleep. Ceana lay facing him, her smooth forehead even with his lips. She was so near that every rock of the cart bumped them against each other.

"Are you awake?" she whispered into his neck.

Her warm breath brushed his skin, and his pulse spiked. He'd never been this close to a woman who wasn't blood before. His mind might feel one way about her, but his treacherous body felt another. He nodded, his lips accidentally grazing her skin.

She recoiled somehow even though she didn't actually move. "I think we're headed in the wrong direction."

It took effort to pull his thoughts away from how soft her

skin was. "What?" His voice came out with extra gravel he couldn't control.

With her top arm, she pointed above their heads. "If we were traveling towards the northern lochs, the sun should be setting on our right." She poked a thumb to the left of the wagon. "But it's setting that way."

Christ defend them. They'd gambled based on what the man had been hawking that the fishmonger had come from the northern system of lochs down to Dunvegan. Instead it seemed he'd come up from the southern lochs. They couldn't stay in the cart if it was taking them farther from Duntulm Castle and Lady MacDonald.

"How many coins have we left?" Ceana asked. "Perhaps we could pay him to take us there?"

His Adam's apple seemed to stick down between his collarbones. "I left most all of what we had to repay the people for the clothes we took."

She tilted her head back and stared into his eyes. Her brown eyes darkened to a shade of black.

He'd hurt her before by doing the wrong thing and hurt her now in his attempt to do the right thing. He should have been used to it, but her disappointment still wrapped around his heart like a noose. "We'll have to get out and pray we've gone far enough to throw the dogs off long enough for us to reach Duntulm."

She broke eye contact. "You first. I'm not climbing over you."

He inched forward, worm-like, and slithered onto his side until he could wrap himself around the barrel behind him. He used it to push himself forward so he faced the open back of the cart. His foot connected with something, and Ceana grunted loudly. It seemed impossible the fishmonger hadn't heard her. He didn't wait to find out or look back to see where he'd kicked her.

He twisted his body and rolled free of the barrels and right off the end of the cart. He smashed into the ground and continued to roll. Dirt stung his eyes and ground between his teeth.

He stopped and sat up. Ceana was already on her feet. She stalked off the dirt path and headed up the grassy hill that butted up against it.

He scrambled after her. "Do you even know if you're headed in the right direction?"

She slammed to a stop. Her chest heaved. "You had no right."

"It's done now, and I can't take it back. It was only a few coins."

"You had no right."

She emphasized each word so strongly that he wasn't sure they were talking only about the coins anymore.

A fish scale stuck to her right cheekbone. He reached for it.

She swatted his hand away before he made contact. "Don't touch me."

"I didn't touch you." Fever-like warmth flushed up the back of his neck and into his face. Nor had he refused to give her the potion, or forced her to take the wishes upon herself, or let her drown. "It's not fair to keep punishing me for things I didn't yet do, especially when you've no way of knowing if I would have done them or not."

She swiped the fish scale off her cheek. "You gave away the last of our money without asking me."

"It was the right thing to do."

"The right thing to do is whatever it takes to remove this curse." She looked like she wanted to shove him but couldn't stand to touch him even that briefly. "Which way's Duntulm Castle?"

She headed off—only half in the right direction—without waiting for his answer.

The warmth built into a ball behind his eyes until it almost blurred his vision. He ground his heel into the earth. He didn't expect her to thank him for what he was sacrificing to help her because she'd also sacrificed for him, but if he was going to suffer the wrath of the fae for her, he at least deserved to know why she hated him. No more half-veiled accusations.

He blocked her path. "I'm not taking you farther until you tell me one thing I'm guilty for. One thing I actually did other than give away a few coins."

She stayed out of his reach, like she had practice evading angry men. "You did the one thing I begged you not to do. You broke your promise."

He ran through the dream in his mind and the time since they'd met again. "I didn't promise you anything."

"Is that what you'll tell yourself after you abandon me this time as well?" The muscles in her throat tightened like she was trying to swallow and couldn't. "I'm the *eejit* here for not taking warning from the first time. I knew better. But my brother..." She shook her head.

Frustration cascaded inside him. It seemed unreasonable for her to hold a promise he'd made in their past life against him now, but that had to be the case. "All I know of our past together is what's in the dream. When did I make this supposed promise?"

"It happened that night, so it's in the dream. There's no point pretending you don't know." Ceana's voice was a tangle of angry and sad and confused. The streaks of reds, purples, and oranges in the sunset behind her seemed to mirror her emotions. "The fairy said the wishes would take over when we both fell asleep. You swore to me that we'd take turns staying awake until we found a way to break the curse. Then you went to sleep anyway."

He ground his fingers into his forehead. So that's what was at the bottom of her anger toward him. It wasn't that they'd almost drowned. She'd been willing to give up her wishes for him even after that. It wasn't that he allowed her to take the curse on herself and give him the blessing of the wishes. They'd been friends even after that.

It was that he'd been the person she trusted most, and then when she most needed him, he failed her. She had no good reason to believe he'd keep his promise this time, and that old sting of betrayal spilled over to color everything he did.

Worse, he couldn't even trust himself.

He almost hadn't gone after her when his dadaidh and Tavish took her away. It was possible he'd grown tired of fighting to keep the wishes from taking effect, or that he'd decided to take them for himself and break his promise. It was also possible he'd simply fallen asleep despite his best intentions.

And, in the end, it didn't matter if it was intentional or not. It almost made it worse if it wasn't because, to her, it must seem that she couldn't trust him to keep his promises even when he intended to.

Somehow, he had to prove to both of them that wasn't the case. The task seemed more monumental than finding a cure for a fae curse. "It's not in my dream, and that's all the memory I have of before the wishes. The dream ends the moment the fairy vanishes."

"She left out your promise? Why would she do that?" She paced in front of him as if she couldn't decide whether to stay with him or cut her losses and leave. She skidded to a stop. "Unless it would make you unhappy. Like the little boy in Dunvegan." She slowly lifted her gaze to his face. "It would have made you unhappy?"

It would have made him unhappy. It did make him unhappy. "Aye, but that doesn't change what happened."

"It might." Her eyes smiled at him even though her lips didn't. "A little. For me."

The words trickled down into his core. It wasn't forgiveness, but it was a start.

For a second, the idea of reaching for her hand crossed his mind, as if taking her hand was something he'd done before. Instead he stuffed his hands under his cloak. "Come on. We have ground to make up."

CHAPTER 12

A hound baying jerked Ceana awake. She squinted against the darkness. It took her three breaths before she remembered where she was—Duntulm Castle lay across a field and up a hill from where they'd camped.

During their travel, the full moon had passed, and the waning moon was covered by clouds and barely gave off enough light to see by. As hard as she squinted, she couldn't make out any forms moving nearby in the darkness. With the way sound traveled at night, they could still be beyond her ability to see them even in daylight—assuming it hadn't been all in her dreams. She'd gone to sleep afraid that Tavish and Allan would catch them so close to Duntulm Castle that the defeat would be twice as bitter.

If she hadn't dreamed the dog's howl, as close as they were to Duntlm Castle might not be close enough. Last night, they camped within sight of the walls but stopped short because the castle gates had been barred for the night before they'd arrived.

The hound bayed again.

She rolled over, planted her hand atop Gavran's mouth, and shook him awake.

He sat straight up, almost smashing his head against hers. She pressed a finger to her lips and lowered her hand. The dog howled closer this time.

They grabbed their cloaks and sprinted from the ring of bushes where they'd camped.

They cut through a fallow field, and another where the spring barley barely brushed the front of her boots even though summer was upon them. By this time of year, it should have been near to her knees. Patches lay withered and yellow.

The hulking mass of Duntulm, the MacDonalds' castle, rose up on the top of the cliff from the gloom. The four-story-tall tower looked like an angry giant, ready to crush them with a house-sized fist. Briny air from the sea beyond filled her lungs and nipped her cheeks.

She slid to a stop, her calves and thighs on fire from the uphill run. "Gavran, wait. How do we get inside?"

His shadow rose and fell in the dark ahead of her, as if he were breathing heavily too. "We'll tell the guards we're running from our disapproving families."

They were running from disapproving families, though they'd never been lovers the way his story implied. It would only work if the guards believed it. "Does the Lady MacDonald provide sanctuary for such couples?"

Gavran motioned her forward, and they stumbled up the last fifty feet of the hill. "I heard a rumor last fall about a couple who eloped to MacDonald castle."

A deep ditch with a single plank across it separated them from the curtain wall and the guardhouse.

Her breathing hitched. She'd climb any tree, but this was different. She couldn't see the bottom. It reminded her of a pit leading straight into hell, and she hadn't been on speaking terms with the Almighty since the curses. Maybe she wasn't as ready and willing to die as she'd thought. And especially not when freedom from the curses might be within her grasp.

Gavran guided her onto the plank. "Don't look down."

"Why do people always say that?" She stretched her arms out from her sides for balance. "You do know saying that only guarantees I will, don't you?"

She reached the middle. The plank quivered beneath her. Her head spun, and she froze. If only they'd made it to the castle a few hours earlier, they could have crossed the regular bridge and been safe inside by now.

"You can do it," Gavran called behind her.

"How certain are you?"

"You're almost there."

She shook her head, immediately regretted the movement,

and edged forward again. "How certain are you about Lady MacDonald providing sanctuary?"

"Half. I'm sure of the rumor, but I don't know how much truth it held."

The hound's calls seemed to be right on top of them, and the rhythmic thumping of cantering horses joined it.

Her feet hit the solid ground. She gasped in a breath and planted her hands on her knees. "Half is better than what I have to offer."

"It's all we have." He bounded across the plank. His teeth flashed in the darkness. "Besides, that's as sure as I was you were telling me the truth when I cut you from the tree." He pounded on the watch door. "And we've no other options."

Fair enough true. Gavran had a sense about people she'd never had. He never forgot a neighbor's name or something they'd told him in all the time she knew him. She'd always been better with problem-solving than with people.

The watch door slid open, and Gavran gave them the story. She held her breath. She could see the horses outlined against the treeline below.

"You'll have to wait until morning," the guard said.

A shout carried on the night air. They'd been spotted.

She ducked under Gavran's arm and pressed her face as close to the guard window as possible. It was at the perfect level for Gavran, but only her eyes could peer over the top. A bearded face looked back at her. The ale and garlic on his breath made her eyes water.

"Please." She wrapped her hands around the bars. "They'll have us dragged back home by then."

The guard nodded to someone behind him, and chains rattled. "I'll let ya in, but you'll have to spend the rest of the night in the dungeon."

EVERY SPEECH SHE'D TRIED TO PREPARE FOR LADY MACDONALD sounded like she should be locked up for madness or cast out for trickery.

Ceana leaned her cheek against the damp stones next to the tiny slat on the locked door so she could see down the hallway. The guard who'd put them in the cell had left a single torch burning at the end. It'd almost burned down now. There couldn't be much left to the night, and she was no further ahead. She shouldn't have rejected Gavran's offer to help her figure out how best to phrase their plea to Lady MacDonald.

It joined her list of the many, many things she shouldn't have done. Her brain couldn't even properly focus on what she'd soon say to Lady MacDonald. Even now, days later, it was too full with replaying her argument with Gavran.

She slapped a hand against the stones. Behind her, Gavran groaned in his sleep.

She turned around to face where he slept, sitting up, his head tilted back against the wall. She pressed her fingers into the stone behind her and dug for the hatred that had grown like mold inside her during her time living under the curses, but she couldn't find it. It seemed to have been burned away and wiped clean.

In its place, the truth lay bare and stark, leaving her nowhere to turn to avoid it.

Rather than clinging to her memories of their years of friendship the way she should have, she'd held on to the one thing he'd done wrong. She'd been trying to punish him for it ever since they'd reunited. It wasn't fair of her.

She didn't know what to say or do to make it right. Apologies had always felt empty to her—mere words and words cost little. Her dadaidh had been master of apologies to her mamaidh when he sobered from the drink.

Apologies and excuses and promises he'd never keep. Those didn't mend a wound any more than thank yous paid a fiddler.

She wasn't even sure she could do it—apologize, forgive him, start again. It was safer to rely on herself.

It was safer to rely on herself because then nobody could let her down. When she hadn't expected her dadaidh to be responsible and take care of her, she wasn't disappointed and left wanting when he wasted his time and their money on drink. If she'd relied on him instead of herself, they all would have starved.

It was safer to rely on herself because then she didn't have to suffer the consequences of anyone else's bad choices when they refused to listen to the potential dangers she spotted in their plans. At least when she decided to walk out into the loch that night to collect cockles, the trouble she'd gotten into had been of her own making. She hadn't been dragged out there by someone else who hadn't been willing to listen to what might go wrong.

It was safer to rely on herself because no one looked on her with pity and thought her weak. She didn't end up pleading for help, leaving her feeling naked while fully clothed. There were no sighs that said they didn't want to help her but felt obligated to.

It was safer, but her stubborn self-reliance was also what got them into this in the first place. She was here now because she went out into the lochs collecting cockles alone, insisting she had to do it by herself. If she'd accepted Gavran's help that night—asked for it even—they might have reached the shore safely on their own.

More than the wishes, her refusal to trust anyone but herself might have been what cost her the best friend she ever had.

She didn't want to be that person anymore. She just wasn't sure how to change it.

Gavran snorted, jerked upright, and rubbed a hand over his face. "Was I asleep? Why didn't you wake me?"

She pressed close to the wall at her back, her hands behind

her. "You deserved some rest, and we've no idea what the morrow will bring."

He stared at her in a way that made her feel like all her thoughts were playing across her face.

"What's wrong?" he asked. She thought he might have smiled, but the lighting was too dim for her to tell for sure. "Other than the obvious."

It wasn't fair that he still knew her so well when he couldn't even remember her. "I don't know what to say to Lady MacDonald."

It wasn't the full truth, but it was as much truth as she was brave enough to share.

He patted the floor beside him.

She crossed the cell slowly and lowered herself down next to him, leaving enough space so that their arms didn't touch. "If I get it wrong—"

"You won't. You'll know what to say when the time comes."

"How can you be so sure? Words tend to abandon me when I need them most."

He dropped his wrists over his knees. "What did you say to the boy? Back in the market."

The two hardly seemed related, but a smile filled her heart at the memory. One bannock was a far cry from what she longed to give him, but it'd been something. It'd made her feel like herself again. She'd seen him there so many times since the curses took hold of her, and she'd never been able to do anything to ease his suffering. "I told him the bannock was from his guardian angel and to remember that the angels of children see the Lord's face in heaven."

"Why tell him that?"

Because she knew what he needed to hear. That must be Gavran's point. When she needed to, she'd know what to say to Lady MacDonald as well.

Gavran was still watching her as if he wanted to hear her answer, though. "To give him hope. When every day's a fight, sometimes hope's all you have to keep you going."

He stiffened beside her. "Ceana."

Her name came out soft. Kay-na. Same as he used to say it when they'd had a quarrel in their teens and he wanted to mend it.

And it choked her. She swallowed hard against a lump that wouldn't give.

He shifted, angling toward her a fraction. Darkness hid his face. "Please forgive—"

She clamped her hand over his mouth. Their private signal. Forgiveness offered. Forgiveness accepted. Maybe some part of him would remember and hear all the things she was too weak to say. "I'm the one—"

He put his hand over her mouth, and her heart thrummed in her ears, so loud something must be wrong with it. He smiled against her palm, and she lowered her hand.

He leaned back against the wall again. Then, quickly, as if he wanted to do it before he could talk himself out of it, he scooted closer and slid an arm around her shoulders.

She should pull away. Her body didn't respond to the command.

Her body might have forgotten, but the woman who once loved him was the old her. She wasn't looking for that from him now. All she wanted now was help and forgiveness and maybe even friendship.

Since they both intended only that, maybe there was no reason to pull away.

Besides, it'd be insulting to reject his olive branch. And after all, the night would only grow colder before it got warm. There was no fire here to stave off the chill.

She leaned into him and rested her head on his shoulder.

It was the most practical thing to do.

CHAPTER 13

A door rattled down the hallway, and Ceana scuttled to her feet. Her legs felt stiff from sitting on the hard floor, and a hazy feeling still filled her brain from lack of rest. The light now streaming down the hallway suggested they'd slept away part of the morning.

It couldn't bode well that Lady MacDonald had waited so long to send for them.

A different guard from the one who'd brought them down the night before unlocked the door. "Lady MacDonald extends her apologies for leaving you waiting so long."

The guard led them through a narrow passageway between buildings, open on the top but lined with stone walls on both sides, and out into the inner courtyard. Ceana blinked against the sun.

Sizzling rose from their left, where venison roasted on a

giant spit over an open flame. The rich scent of roasting red meat, fennel, and rosemary hung heavy in the air, and Ceana's mouth watered. It was no wonder her body felt held together by nothing more than her dirty clothes. She and Gavran hadn't had anything to eat but what they could forage since the bannocks Gavran bought the morning they went to the spaewife. That was days ago.

A little boy, carrying a stack of wood high enough that only half his face showed, stared at them on their way by.

The guard let them into the main building. The woman waiting inside with another guard had exotic skin, like the Middle Eastern trader Ceana had once seen bringing silk to Dunvegan Castle, and hair and eyes the color of a seal's pelt. The blue of her dress matched the depths of the ocean and seemed to flow around her.

She didn't hold out her arms. She didn't smile. She didn't introduce herself or welcome them. Yet the overwhelming urge to hide in her embrace and cry on her shoulder nearly drove Ceana to her knees. Like she'd find peace there. She couldn't explain it. Even as a child, she'd been the one to hold her mamaidh when she cried, not the other way around.

"My guards tell me you're running from your families." Lady MacDonald's voice—it had to be Lady MacDonald—carried the same soothing quality as waves lapping at the shore. It was the type of voice people wanted to listen to. "And there are two distraught men in my courtyard who claim you're a witch who's cast a spell on him."

Gavran gave the kind of awkward smile that was the only appropriate response to something horribly embarrassing.

Ceana felt her own face freeze into a matching smile. One of them had to tell her the truth. She flicked a glance to Gavran, but he just stood there, following her firm insistence from when they were first tossed in the cell that she wanted to be the one to speak. She should have remembered to retract that order.

"My priest will wed you." The corners of Lady MacDonald's eyes crinkled. "I hope you'll share the story behind that accusation with me during your stay."

The words played hide-and-seek with her tongue. She closed her eyes against the immensity of it. The wrong words and Lady MacDonald would send them away. But what words could convince a highborn lady, even one rumored to have had dealings with the fae in the past, that she spoke true about her curse?

Gavran nudged her.

She forced her eyes open. Both Gavran and Lady MacDonald watched her.

All signs of mirth had vanished from Lady MacDonald's face. She swept her hand toward a doorway behind her. "It seems I need to hear the story now."

They entered the room as directed, followed by Lady MacDonald and the two guards.

"Sit," Lady MacDonald said.

Ceana obediently dropped into the nearest chair. After so long not speaking of her curse, to have to share it with Gavran and a stranger who could decide her fate in such a short period of time left her backbone feeling a touch wobbly. She swallowed until the dryness in her throat eased. "I'm not a witch, but I am cursed by the fae."

"I understand how confusing it can be if his family has told him you're cursed in order to keep you apart." Lady MacDonald's voice took on that exhausted, longsuffering tone of a parent explaining something to their child for the tenth time. "The fae meddle in human affairs far less often than people believe. I assure you that most so-called curses are superstition and nothing more."

Just once she'd like someone to believe her—believe in her. "Why is it everyone thinks we're daft?"

Gavran glanced at her with a look that said he wasn't sure whether she was asking him or Lady MacDonald, but that she might, in fact, be daft for snapping her tongue at a lady.

She folded her hands in her lap. She had to keep this in perspective. What Lady MacDonald thought of her, or of them, or of anyone else didn't matter so long as she helped them in the end. And she had at least admitted that some fae curses were real. That meant they simply had to show her they weren't like all the other people who, based on her tone of voice, had come pounding on her door claiming fae troubles. "We don't wish to marry. My curse is no mere superstition."

In as balanced a voice as she could manage, she explained how the fairy pulled them from the water and the condition of the wishes. She included every detail she could remember, including how the fairy's touch felt like sand draining through her fingers. No telling what piece of information might make the difference. She took the story right up until they found out the truth of her brother's condition.

"I don't know where my brother is or if he has enough food to fill his belly. I can't find him and care for him with the curse of the wishes blocking everything I try to do."

The expression on Lady MacDonald's face was too controlled, like she was listening out of politeness. "That is a sad tale, but I'm uncertain what you want from me."

Gavran leaned forward. "We heard you'd had dealings with the fae in the past. We need your help to remove the curse."

"Even *if* you have a real curse, you've been misled." A muscle in Lady MacDonald's cheek pulsed, then stilled. "I've no special powers to remove it."

The floor seemed to drop out from under Ceana. She grasped the arms of the chair to keep from tipping forward. That was the end of it, then. If Lady MacDonald wouldn't believe them and couldn't help them, surely no one else could.

"I'm sorry I couldn't have been of more help," Lady MacDonald said.

Gavran rose and lifted Ceana to her feet. Lady MacDonald turned from them and headed for the door.

Gavran tilted his face close to Ceana's ear. "I think she's lying. Is there anything else you can tell her?"

She'd given Lady MacDonald all the facts. She shouldn't have bothered. She'd known this was futile. She ought to have died in the streets of Dunvegan rather than allowing Gavran to drag her halfway across the isle.

"Something in her face when she said she can't help." His lips were back by her ear, insisting she listen, insisting she focus. "She can help us, but she doesn't wish to. Or she's afraid to."

Lady MacDonald seemed like many things, but *afraid* wasn't one of them. Gavran had always been able to see things in people that she hadn't, though.

Fear was a powerful force. Logical arguments and simple pleas for help were no match for it. Only eliciting another, stronger emotion, like love or empathy, might have a chance.

She couldn't make Lady MacDonald love her with a few words, but she might be able to make her desire to show mercy and compassion.

She pulled away from Gavran's hold and grabbed for Lady MacDonald's arm. "Wait."

The pointy-faced guard snapped a hand around her wrist before her fingers could so much as brush the fabric of the lady's sleeve and yanked her to the side. He flicked his free hand in Gavran's direction and the other guard drew his sword and laid the tip against Gavran's chest. "We'll toss them out, my lady."

Ceana squirmed in his grip so she had a clear view of Lady

MacDonald's face. Let the guard kill her for it if he must, but she couldn't lose this chance if Gavran was right. "I could handle the hunger and the pain. Saint Paul did. But what it does to you inside—you start to forget why you did it in the first place. You forget what it felt like to believe the Almighty hears you when you pray. It makes you forget who you are. And you are completely alone, unique in the worst possible way. Without hope that anything you do will matter." She struggled against the guard's hold, but he hauled her farther back. "Help us. Me. Help me."

"I'm truly sorry." Lady MacDonald shook her head, but the movement looked painful. "I cannot."

"What would you have us do with them, my lady?" the pointy-faced guard asked.

"Take them back to the dungeon for now while I decide whether to turn them over to his family or set them free."

CHAPTER 14

S alome MacDonald reached into the recesses of her soul,
searching with her mind for the well of inner peace
that used to be her birthright. Like so many other
things she'd lost when she traded her immortality for a
numbered human existence, her peace was gone. She'd rarely
faced a dilemma serious enough to need it since she'd made her
decision to become human. And she, as yet, had no idea how to
function without it.

She eased open the door into Ihon's study. He leaned over his
desk with a piece of parchment spread out in front of him. A
goose quill pen swung from his fingers like a pendulum. He
dipped the end of the quill into his ink pot and touched it to the
paper. The earthiness of the soft scratching wrapped around her
like an embrace but couldn't quite chase away the unease that
held her mind captive.

He glanced up but didn't stop writing. "I've bad news. Hugh sent word he'll be joining us for an extended visit no later than week's end."

She rubbed at a knot of tension in her shoulder. Hugh's visits were unwelcome enough when she didn't also have a nuckalevee and a new potential problem to cope with. Now any decision they made would need to be made under the pressure of his impending arrival. "I've placed a couple under watch in the dungeon, my lord husband."

He grunted. "I'll have the captain of the guard see they receive the appropriate punishment."

She would have Ihon's full attention once he knew the extent of it. They rarely spoke of her past and what she truly was. Only her doctor knew she'd once been fae, and they couldn't risk a servant overhearing. Even though she was now human and most of the powers she once had were gone, many would still try to use her.

She let him finish writing his current sentence so he wouldn't forget whatever was of such great import. "They might be unseelie."

His quill slipped across the page and left an unsightly black blotch where it landed. His body went still.

"The girl asked me to remove a curse and described a seelie fae more accurately than any mortal should have been able to."

She'd also described Salome's feelings—nearly unconscious until she'd heard them spoken aloud—about the decision she'd made. Almost as if the young woman sought to make her recant.

He let the quill fall and swiveled in his chair to face her. "A dungeon won't hold unseelie fae."

"I've set it as a test." She reached for the well of peace again and hit only emptiness. She would have to figure out how to make decisions without direction from the Lord God, without certainty that the choice she made was right. "I've had them placed in the cell nearest the smithy. With so much iron nearby, they won't hold their human form for long. If they're unseelie, they'll need to leave or, by tomorrow morn, be exposed for what they are."

"We should execute them now. We've been patient enough, letting the nuckalevee stunt our crops and spread the plague. I won't have more unseelie invading our very home."

She rested a hand on his arm. His solution was tempting, but the deal they'd made to allow them to be together forbade her from interfering in the war currently raging between the fae seelie and unseelie courts or from directly attacking another fae, even if that fae were an unseelie bent on harming humanity like the nuckalevee. In forsaking her spot among the seelie fae, she'd lost the right to involve herself in their affairs.

She'd lost much more than she realized she would. "We don't know yet if they're unseelie. If they aren't, we would be unjust, and if they are, executing them would violate the agreement we made."

"And you're certain confining them overnight will show their nature?"

"Patience and discipline aren't qualities of the unseelie. Their frustration at their failure to bait me into making them a promise would make it difficult for them to maintain enough control to hold their human forms even without the iron. We'll know with certainty by dawn."

"Isn't the nuckalevee enough?" Ihon scrubbed at the bridge of his nose. His voice was low and tired. "Why would unseelie come here with this ruse?"

"I assume as another attempt to draw me out since we haven't reacted to the nuckalevee's presence. The unseelie don't know for certain how much or how little of my power remains to me. They can't know I'm unable to remove a curse. Had I made a direct promise to remove the curse from them, the unseelie could have argued to the seelie court that I'd broken the agreement and should suffer the consequences."

Ihon clenched the arms of his chair. "The seelie court demanded a steep price in exchange for allowing us to be together."

"Nothing with the fae is ever free." She moistened her lips with the tip of her tongue. Ceana Campbell's words still sang a cadence in her head. *You start to forget why you did it in the first place. You forget what it felt like to believe the Almighty hears you when you pray.* The girl could have been talking about Salome rather than herself. "Do you think the price too steep?"

He took her hand in his, kissed each of her knuckles in turn, and shook his head. "But it pains me to have to watch our people suffer. At least they don't recognize the cause. Knowing a monster plagued them would only create panic and false accusations." He squeezed her hand. "If you're not sure they're unseelie, why lock them up? Why not send them on their way, unseelie or not?"

"They claim a fairy cursed them."

"What did they do to provoke her?"

"Nothing, so they say." She told him the story Ceana had told her.

Ihon frowned and rose to his feet. "They must be lying. Fairies are seelie, aren't they?"

So much knowledge that she took for granted that humanity as yet didn't share. "Not all. It's extremely rare, but some have fallen from grace. Those that have are the most dangerous, for they're like the Deceiver, able to disguise themselves as angels of light."

She moved his quill from the parchment and cleaned off the ink that had leaked out to cover the staff. She hadn't yet become comfortable with writing the human way. Teaching her hand to hold the quill correctly and draw the tip along at the right speed and pressure to form words, it was all so difficult compared to etching a message into stone with nothing but a thought or signaling an event of great import in the sky with the stars. When she struggled, Ihon tried to console her with the idea that human women rarely knew how to read or write, but she couldn't bear the thought of not being his equal as she should be.

She laid the clean quill next to the ink bottle and capped the bottle to prevent a worse spill. She kept her back turned to him. "If they speak true, however, it means the war escalates. The seelie should have removed the wishes and the curses that came along with them within minutes. These two should have woken thinking it'd all been but a nightmare. That they did not means other, more serious things occupied the attention of the seelie court."

They'd suspected the same thing when the nuckalevee appeared weeks ago and was allowed to roam unchecked, but it prevented her from traveling to reach her contact. She had no way of confirming what was happening or of letting the seelie fae know so they could balance the scales. Even alerting the seelie fae to the nuckalevee could have been construed as violating her agreement, but her contact was an old friend who valued the spirit of the law over the letter.

Muscular arms wrapped around her and drew her into an embrace. "It's beyond our control."

She drew in a deep breath of his scent, like saltwater and wet sand. Like home. "What of the man and woman in our dungeon? If they prove to be human rather than unseelie—"

"You can't help them. We'll give them whatever physical aid we can, food, money, but that's all we can do."

She was helpless to personally remove the curse from Ceana, but perhaps they shouldn't send them away, either. She, better than anyone else, knew how Ceana felt. In a way, they were kindred. It was possible a deal could be the solution to both of their troubles. "I believe we can help each other. I'll tell them I'll introduce them to one who has the power to help them, but that they need to kill the nuckalevee for me first."

Ihon's arms tightened spastically around her middle. "Nae. I won't risk losing you. You can't be involved."

"I won't be. They're not in our employ, and I won't be the one lifting the curse from them."

"Still. Two untrained peasants against a monster..."

She could almost hear him thinking *should we trade two lives to try to save two thousand?* From his perspective, it would seem like a direct trade.

It makes you forget who you are, Ceana had said. *And you are completely alone, unique in the worst possible way.* Even with all she'd told him, Ihon still couldn't grasp exactly what was at stake in the war between the seelie and unseelie. She'd almost allowed herself to forget. She'd almost wanted to forget. "It may be the only chance we have to rid ourselves of the nuckalevee."

And strike a blow against the unseelie court.

"In truth, what help could you offer them?" he asked. "We

can't in good conscience ask them to risk their lives if we have no reward to give should they, by some miracle, succeed."

Ihon was right. Even fifty trained men would be unlikely to slay a nuckalevee. Yet perhaps she'd still be doing at least Ceana a kindness. A true fae curse was a harsh burden. Better she die quickly from the nuckalevee than suffer for years to come.

"I can have my contact lodge a petition with the seelie court." She couldn't guarantee Eliezer would take her request to the court, but Ceana and Gavran had no other option. No one but the seelie court could annul the wishes and the curse that came with them. All the cures sold by humans for supposed fae curses were nothing more than poison or smoke and empty promises. "The court may choose not to act on it, but it will be more to hope for than what these two will find anywhere else."

Ihon kissed her neck and released her. "At the very least, we'll need to train them before sending them out."

"It will need to be you. No one else can know. If it's to be done, it must be done quickly and quietly before the unseelie court has a chance to catch word of it. And before Hugh's arrival complicates matters further."

CHAPTER 15

Gavran leaned back against the cold stone of the cell and scrubbed his hands through his hair. Nothing he did reached Ceana. She'd lain on the damp floor all night. Red ringed her eyes, but she hadn't cried. In fact, she hadn't done anything. Or said anything. He'd promised to help her find her freedom, and they'd ended up in a different cage.

The door at the end of the hall rattled, and light washed down the corridor. The door to their cell creaked open next.

Lady MacDonald and her two guards entered.

On the floor at his feet, Ceana's head shifted, just enough that he was sure she saw Lady MacDonald but not enough that it couldn't have been a mere reflex. Then her body curved in on itself. It reminded him of the roly poly bugs, so vulnerable when stretched out but absolutely impenetrable when they curl into a ball, only their solid shell exposed to the world.

He stepped in front of Ceana, blocking her from Lady MacDonald's view. "My lady—"

Lady MacDonald held up her hand and left it there, suspended in mid-air like a blocker. She angled her head so that her profile faced Gavran, and her gaze commanded the attention of her guards. "Please leave us."

The taller guard, with the pointy face, rocked back and forth, and the older guard's gaze hopped between Ceana and the door.

Lady MacDonald lowered her hand and turned the full force of her unnaturally calm gaze onto Gavran. "We had a misunderstanding earlier, but they're no threat to me. True, yes?"

The *yes* hit Gavran's ears funny. Foreign. Like her appearance and mannerisms. "We came to seek your help, not your harm."

Both guards murmured *Aye, my lady* and backed out the door.

Lady MacDonald's gaze flickered past him, toward the floor. "A fairy curse can't be broken by any human means. I spoke true before when I told you I couldn't provide what you sought."

A small sound escaped from Ceana. He glanced back. She still lay curled into a ball.

He dropped to his knees beside her. His own pious platitudes in the past about failure making a person stronger and providing a learning opportunity for future success taunted him now. Ceana had been right. He'd never known true failure. And this kind of failure didn't bear the bitterness of medicine, bringing healing along with the sting. It bore the bitterness of fetid meat, sickening him with every bite.

He wasn't sure Ceana would rally this time. Everyone had a point where their spirit could take no more punishment.

He looked back up at Lady MacDonald. "Is there nothing we can do? No one else you could send us to?"

Lady MacDonald sighed, more deeply than seemed possible and looked again at Ceana. "Please encourage her to sit. I have a proposal, but I won't make it until I know you're both willing to hear it. I suspect she's had enough choices taken from her since the curse."

Ceana moved on the ground beside him. She gave him a fragile look. He hated not being able to stand between her and whatever Lady MacDonald might have to say.

He offered her his hand, and she took it. They both stood. At least they wouldn't have to look up at Lady MacDonald that way.

Ceana dropped his hand but stayed next to him.

"I can't cure the curse," Lady MacDonald said, "but I have a connection who may be able to aid you. Unlike you and me, he's not human."

A strange pain rattled in his chest like something vital had shaken loose. Perhaps, after all of this, he shouldn't have been surprised to hear it confirmed that the fae existed, but part of him still was. "He's fae?"

The lady nodded. "But you will never find him without my help, and he will not reveal himself to you unless I'm with you."

He well knew the change that happened in a voice during a marketplace haggle. Lady MacDonald's voice sounded that way now. "And what will such help cost us? We have no money. Nothing of value to offer."

"We have no want or need for your money. What I need is a service from you."

Ceana stiffened beside him, and he spread his feet, bracing for what was to come.

"What type of service?" Ceana asked.

Her voice was spread thin with suspicion. He moved closer to her so their sleeves brushed. He'd expected her to jump at the offer with no questions asked. But with all she'd suffered in the time before he found her, perhaps he shouldn't be surprised she regarded the lady's words with more caution than even he did.

The lady's lips quivered as if they wanted to smile, but she wouldn't give them the freedom. "My contact can't be reached by letter or messenger. He'll show himself to me alone, and at present, I'm a prisoner in my own home. Because of my knowledge of the fae, they've sent a nuckalevee to kill me should I ever leave the castle grounds."

Gavran traded a glance with Ceana. Christ preserve them. The fae were more malicious even than the tales told.

Ceana tilted her chin up. "And you want us to do what, exactly?"

"I want you to kill it."

Gavran ground his teeth together to keep from cursing. Lady

MacDonald had a castle full of trained soldiers, yet she chose to send them against whatever a nuckalevee was. "Why don't your guards kill it?"

She smiled this time, but it was more of a movement of muscle than an actual sign of mirth. "My husband believes that if we directly attack it, it will anger the fae further. If someone else were to slay it, there would be no repercussions."

For the MacDonalds at least, but what about them? His mamaidh feared the power of a fae as small as a water spriggan. "What's a nuckalevee?"

Ceana shifted. "According to my mamaidh's stories, it looks like a one-eyed horse. With no skin." The hand next to his brushed his fingers. "Crops wither in its path, and its breath spreads disease wherever it goes."

No wonder his mamaidh refused to tell the old myths and stories. Neither of his sisters would sleep if they thought a skin-less horse roamed the countryside, waiting to afflict them with the Black Death or whatever other pestilence struck its fancy. "Is that truth?"

The lady watched Ceana with narrowed eyes. "Yes."

Gavran scrubbed a finger across his upper lip. It was moist. "Then how do you expect us to kill a supernatural beast? Can a fae even die?"

One side of her mouth quirked again. "They can't die, but they can be banished from this world by killing their physical form, and that, more precisely, is what I ask of you. Once you return it to the spirit realm, it will be locked away in Tartarus, and it won't be able to return to this earth until the end of days."

Slaughtering a cow or a sheep was easy, but a supernatural monster like Lady MacDonald described would be more like a bear. He'd seen men mauled to death trying to rid themselves of a bear who'd gotten a taste for their livestock. He shifted his gaze to the lady again. "I'm sure you don't kill a monster with an arrow or an axe."

"If they're made of iron."

He wanted to lower his head into his hands and block out everything. A month ago, he wouldn't have believed any of this existed. Now he was tied to a woman cursed by a fairy, had learned his whole life was the way it was because he was blessed by three wishes, and he was being asked to believe that he could kill a supernatural beast with a simple iron weapon.

Instead of burying his face, he straightened. "Why iron?"

Something flickered across the lady's face that he couldn't interpret. It almost looked like respect. "You've heard the tale that iron will keep fae away?"

He nodded.

"For once, the stories are true. When the Lord God created the fae, he put safeguards in place to limit their power because some were predestined to fall. One of those safeguards is iron."

Something about it all still didn't sit right, but he couldn't be sure if it was because his instincts were telling him Lady MacDonald played them false or if it was that some baser part of him sought a reason to leave with the wishes intact. Perhaps a bit of both. His feelings couldn't be trusted.

Ceana's feet pointed towards the door, but her upper body leaned toward Lady MacDonald as if a war raged inside her as well over whether to take the offer or run.

His gaze snagged on hers. "Ceana?"

GAVRAN DIDN'T WANT TO TAKE LADY MACDONALD'S OFFER. Ceana could see it in the set of his jaw. Lady MacDonald had given him a perfect excuse to abandon her without feeling guilty.

Angry words kindled in her chest and started to cascade down her tongue, but Gavran's gaze held hers, his face a touch paler than usual.

She clamped her teeth on her bottom lip and swallowed the words down. Gavran wasn't her enemy here. He'd asked wise questions—ones she should have thought to ask—and his fear didn't mean he'd run away. She ought to be more afraid than she was.

Lady MacDonald was the one to be doubted. Ceana broke away from Gavran's gaze and faced Lady MacDonald again. "Won't they send another if we kill this one?"

"Perhaps." Lady MacDonald's expression gave nothing away. "Perhaps not. I am hoping for the latter. And, at the very least, it will give us the time needed to reach my contact."

"What guarantee do we have that you'll keep your word and help us once the nuckalevee is gone?"

"None. You can't speak of this to anyone, nor can we sign an agreement of any kind. You will have to trust me, and I will have to trust you not to share what I've asked of you. If you reveal my connection to the fae, my life may be forfeit as well."

The niggling in her mind wouldn't clear. It poked at her gut and twisted around her lungs, making it hard to draw a clean breath. Trying to trust Gavran was one thing. What Lady MacDonald asked was entirely another. "You could stay safely behind your walls. Why endanger your secrets for us?"

Lady MacDonald rested a hand on her belly. Her gaze settled on Ceana, and for a moment, she looked almost motherly. As quickly as it'd come, her features smoothed out again, and she lowered her hand. "I know what it feels like to make a decision that you would willingly make again and yet which fills you with remorse at the same time. The opportunity you're giving me in slaying the nuckalevee isn't so very different from the opportunity I give to you."

It wasn't the answer she'd expected. And instead of setting her at ease, it set the niggling feeling inside her looping and spiraling again.

Beside her, Gavran heaved in a breath and let it out, out, out.

She didn't need to make this decision on her own. "We need to talk it over before we decide."

Lady MacDonald inclined her head. "I'll give you a few

minutes, but no more. If you wish to accept the offer, we must begin preparations without delay."

She left them alone in their cell. She didn't close the door behind her.

Ceana ran her tongue slowly over her lips and rolled them together. She was no naïve bairn to fall for every tale she was told, and this felt like the tallest tale she'd heard. And yet, if the past few days had taught her anything, it was that she might be too quick to judge and too slow to trust. "Does something feel wrong about this situation to you?"

Gavran cocked an eyebrow at her in a way that said *What doesn't feel wrong about this?*

A laugh built like a geyser inside of her, but she stoppered it before it could escape. Her mamaidh always said she had a touch of the macabre to her. She shouldn't find humor in this. "Do you trust Lady MacDonald?"

Gavran rubbed his eyes. "Harvesting the wheat with the tares. I'm sure there's some truth in what she's told us, but she's sown some lies in as well, so we either have to take the lies with the truth or none at all."

All or none. He was right.

Futile as it might seem, fighting the nuckalevee was at least an actionable goal. No more hunting for elusive answers or stumbling around blind. But they might go through with all Lady MacDonald asked and have no reward to show for it. Or be killed in the attempt. "So then what do you think we should do?"

The words sounded stilted and off-key to her, like playing a fiddle with untrained fingers. Perhaps trust and teamwork weren't something that always came naturally. Perhaps they required practice like anything else.

He flickered a smile like he was trying—unsuccessfully—to set her at ease, and then said nothing for the longest time. When he finally spoke, his voice sounded rusty. "Our question needs to be do we believe she's told us true that she's the only one who can help us and that the nuckalevee has trapped her and is causing the blight and plague? If that's true, we have no choice but to fight the nuckalevee, whether we trust her or not."

But how was she supposed to tell true from false? She'd been wrong about Gavran when she'd given in to her hatred and fool-ishly thought he'd changed when she was the one who'd changed. They'd been taken in by the spaewife, too. "Not all famines and plagues are caused by supernatural evil."

"True enough, but what reason would the MacDonalds have for sending us on a fool's errand if there's no nuckalevee?" Gavran absently rubbed at his shoulder. "If they wanted us gone, they could have turned us over to my dadaidh and been done with it. And I'm certain they're not cruel enough to seek enter-tainment by tormenting us. Even on MacLeod lands, the MacDonalds are spoken of with respect."

"So the nuckalevee is real, or at least the MacDonalds believe it is." If Lady MacDonald spoke true, and she walked away, she'd never get another chance to break the curse. She'd not be able to help her brother. "Do you think she's telling the truth about being our only hope?"

He let out an eternal sigh. "I want to tell you I think we can find another way."

He wanted to, but he didn't. This was the only way. Fight the nuckalevee or give up. "We choose together."

The words still hurt on the way out, but they felt a little more natural than before.

His gaze slid away from her face, and more emotions than she could name or attempt to guess at washed across his features. "If this is the only way, we need to do it, for your sake and for your brother's. And for mine, too. I'm trying to become better at keeping promises than I am at making them."

Her words tossed back at her, but his smile took the sting out of them. "So we fight the nuckalevee?"

He took her hand and she let him—just this once, to seal their agreement. "We fight the nuckalevee."

CHAPTER 16

The walls, lined with *claidheamh-mor* swords, war axes, dirks, and other weapons she'd never seen before, made Ceana feel like she was suffocating. She'd been lucky as a child not to slice off her finger while skinning neeps. She'd like as fall on one of these weapons as be able to wield it well against the nuckalevee.

Gavran strode forward and pulled a *claidheamh-mor* from its hooks on the wall. The sword had a twisted hilt that looked like a unicorn's horn, and decorative clovers capped each end of the curved crossguard.

He drew it from its sheath with a rasp and swung it confidently in a figure-eight pattern. "A handsome weapon."

Lord MacDonald grinned. "Aye. But you won't want to go up against a nuckalevee with a claymore. Long as it is, you'd still be in too close quarters with the beast."

Ceana raised a hand in front of her, stretched her fingers out as long as they would go. She could lay her hands palm to fingertip ten times or more along the length of the blade, yet that would be too close to the nuckalevee?

She straightened her shoulders. She'd not lose courage now. Given the choice of anything over continuing to live with her curse, she'd choose the other option. "What weapons would you have us use? Neither of us have even seen a nuckalevee before."

Lord MacDonald lifted a polearm from the rack next to him. The weapon's long shaft ended in an axe-like blade and spike mounted on the top. On the opposite side from the axe blade was a pointed hook.

Lord MacDonald offered it to her. "A Lochaber axe. The nuckalevee's like a giant horse, and this is the best tool for fighting a mounted opponent."

She hesitated, then grasped the pole with both hands. It swayed slightly in her grip, like a wind caught it even thought they were inside. The head towered over her, more than six feet long in all.

She raised it off the floor, and it bobbed left to right. Gavran and Lord MacDonald jumped back a step. The Lochaber axe wasn't as heavy as she'd expected, but it was awkward.

"Maybe we'll have to saw the bottom off to fit it to your height," Lord MacDonald said.

He motioned for Gavran to grab one as well and headed outside. She followed them, but the end of the Lochabar axe caught on the edge of the door, and she pitched forward over it. She threw out her hands, and the rough stones scraped her palms. She bit back a cry and scrambled to her feet.

The men were far enough ahead that neither of them seemed to notice. She turned away from them and pressed her gritty palms to her eyes. She couldn't fail at this. She couldn't.

She scooped up the Lochabar axe and held it close under the head, dragging the pole along the ground.

The training fields stood empty, and no movement came from the nearby stables. Lady MacDonald had emphasized that they couldn't be tied to what Ceana and Gavran were planning to do, but Ceana hadn't fully understood the lengths they were willing to go to in order to keep their secret. Emptying an entire segment of their castle, especially given the unusual number of children who inhabited the place, must have taken a monumental effort.

A tingle of numbness ran over her. They weren't being sent out like some sort of sacrifice to appease the monster or to keep the secret, were they?

She slapped her palm against the Lochabar pole. The time living under the curse made her expect the worst in every situation. If the MacDonalds expected them to be killed by the nuckalevee, they would have let them go out with swords.

Lord MacDonald staged Gavran through moves with the Lochabar she could barely follow let alone imitate. Gavran picked them up quickly. The MacLeods forced the men on their lands to undergo a certain amount of training when they came of age. She hadn't envied Gavran that at the time, but she did now.

"Your turn," Lord MacDonald called.

She dragged her Lochabar out onto the field. The thing thumped behind her like a broken limb. If she didn't know better, she'd think it mocked her.

"Hold it like this." Lord MacDonald pushed her hands apart. "You'll balance it better with a greater spread."

She increased the distance between her hands.

He grimaced in a way that clearly said *You're not paying attention.* "Not that far. Your shoulders will tire too easily."

Ceana closed her grip until he nodded.

"You need to learn is how to take a blow without losing your grip. You can't take the full force as small as you are. Let it roll off to the side, like water off a tent."

But how was she supposed to do that? Beside her, Gavran swung his Lochabar and cleaved the arm from the straw-stuffed practice dummy. Was this something born into a man? Surely Lord MacDonald realized she had no idea what he meant.

He struck with his Lochabar. She flung hers up to block him. The blow slammed into the middle of her pole, down through her arms, her shoulders, her back, her legs. Her knees buckled, and she dropped the pole, her muscles throbbing.

Lord MacDonald growled. "That's a kiss compared to what a blow from the nuckalevee will feel like. I don't know what

Salome was thinking asking me to train a woman to go up against a beast."

"Then give me a weapon I can actually use." She shoved to her feet and kicked the Lochabar aside. Her dadaidh's face swam before her. She seemed doomed to face man after man who felt she wasn't good enough, wasn't worthy, simply because she was a woman. Maybe she couldn't swing a claymore or control a Lochabar, but she'd learned to hunt to keep food in her family's mouths when her dadaidh was too drunk to do it himself. "I can shoot. Give me a *dorlochis* of arrows, and I'll show you I'm as valuable in a fight as any man."

Lord MacDonald lowered his weapon. "Easy, easy. I intended no offense. If marriage to Salome has taught me anything, it's that a woman is equal in many ways to a man."

For as long as she could recall, she'd wondered if Gavran and his dadaidh were the only ones who saw women as people rather than property. Her face still burned thinking of the way her dadaidh and Robbie Forsyth had bartered over what she was worth as if she wasn't in the same room or was too stupid to comprehend.

Lord MacDonald held out his hand, and she returned the Lochabar to him. "Whatever skills you might have with a bow won't be enough. An arrow can't penetrate the flesh of a nuckalevee."

Gavran stopped his practice swings. "I thought you said it doesn't have skin."

Lord MacDonald shook his head in that slow, sad way Ceana used to think belonged only to a priest telling a family that someone had passed. "It doesn't. But its flesh and veins are tougher than a grizzled bear's hide. It'll take more than an arrow, or even a volley of arrows, to bring it down." He shifted the Lochabar to one hand and placed the other hand on her shoulder with an unexpected gentleness. "Your arrow will feel like nothing more than mosquito bites to the nuckalevee."

What good was a mosquito against a monster? The best she had to offer would be nothing more than an annoyance to it. An annoyance, but perhaps if they worked as a team… "Would it be enough to distract it and give Gavran a better chance at slaying it?"

"Ah!" Lord MacDonald shot a grin at Gavran. "And now you see why I value Salome as well. These women look at things in a way we don't. The Almighty certainly knew what he was doing when he took out Adam's rib to create him a helpmeet."

The memories of her old life rushed back in, like they were drawn to the vacuum created whenever she let go of the hurt of them for even a second. Why had her dadaidh been unable to value her, even though she was only a girl and not the son he wanted her to be?

She bit the inside of her cheek to try to drown out the sting in her heart with an ache elsewhere. It didn't matter anymore. She'd never see her dadaidh again. What she needed to focus on now was freeing herself from her curse so she could build a new life and find her brother. Maybe she'd even be able to wed a man like Lord MacDonald or Gavran's dadaidh who would take her as an equal partner.

"I'll get you a bow to practice with before we go to seek the most likely place to meet the nuckalevee," Lord MacDonald said, "but don't underestimate it. Arrows won't distract it for long. And it will look fragile when you see it, its veins exposed to the light. That's its way of distracting you. It's a fierce predator, with the stamina of ten men, and if you don't kill it quickly, you'll become its next prey."

"Ceana won't underestimate it," Gavran said. "She's smarter than that."

She wrapped her arms around herself and clutched her elbows. She might one day find a man like Lord MacDonald. Or like Gavran.

A lump formed like a tumor in her throat and filled it 'til she thought she'd choke. She didn't hate Gavran anymore, but that didn't mean she had to love him again, either. It'd felt like frostbite charred off half her heart when she lost him before. She didn't want to ever feel that way again, and that's all that could come of allowing herself to care for him now.

He hadn't loved her before the wishes. There was no reason that should change, especially since his family believed she was a witch and he was promised to wed Brighde.

This time, she'd be wise. This time, she'd keep a tight rein on her heart.

CHAPTER 17

Ceana perched astride the horse, following Lord MacDonald and Gavran. Since the nuckalevee only came out after dark, they needed to find and examine the likeliest spots for its arrival in the daylight. They'd spent yesterday training, and tonight they would attack.

Her horse danced, and Ceana grabbed the saddle. Lord MacDonald offered her a side saddle, but she hadn't been able to figure out how to balance with the horse standing still, let alone once it moved. She'd much rather sit solidly, no matter what anyone else thought of her after. She didn't have a reputation left to lose anyway.

In front of her, Gavran looked shakier than she did. Every time the horse shifted under him, he stiffened and yanked on the reins. His mare tossed her head and snorted. Gavran had never been much of a rider. The wishes hadn't changed that.

Lord MacDonald reined in his horse. They caught up with him, and he pointed across the fields.

In the daylight, they looked worse than they had during their evening sprint to the castle. The furrows that should have been green with waves of oats and barley lay fallow.

Feeble curls of smoke rose on the horizon from only a smattering of the cottages.

Lord MacDonald jutted his chin toward them. "They haven't the manpower left to replant this field, even with the extra hands and seed we've sent. Half the families living there and sharing these fields have died from the plague."

According to what Lord MacDonald had told them on the ride, their farmers thought the crops died of some new form of blight. The nuckalevee needed to be stopped before there weren't any harvestable fields remaining. Without at least some harvest, those who survived the plague wouldn't make it through the winter.

A sickeningly sweet taste filled the back of her mouth. She knew what it was like to wake in the morning already worried about how to make stores stretch until the plants began to grow. She knew what it was like to give her portion to someone else so they could sleep for a night without the ache in their belly. Her brain had sometimes become so full with thoughts of making it from one day to the next, giving what small moments of happiness she could to those around her, that she went to bed empty and soul tired, too tired even to pray for a miracle.

Lord MacDonald nudged his horse forward. "The place you're most like to spot the nuckalevee is at the center of where the plague and failed crops are worst."

It made sense. The center of the devastation would be the spot the nuckalevee visited most often.

They rode in silence past fields that had been planted, but the sprouts were yellow and withered. The meadows were empty and too still.

"The nuckalevee, did it do something to the livestock, too?" she asked.

"Aye." Lord MacDonald patted the shoulder of his mare. "Most of the sheep and oxen took sick overnight. Couldn't identify a cause."

Ceana shifted in her seat. Lady MacDonald's claims that they didn't want to further anger the fae suddenly rang false. The people and animals were dying, and the harvest would be too small to feed those who lived. What more harm could the fae do?

A field away, they passed a grove of trees that looked like they'd been burned up but left standing. Their leaves hung brown and crinkled from blackened branches. Her mount snorted and skittered to the side.

"My lord?" she called.

Gavran and Lord MacDonald maneuvered their horses around.

She pointed at the grove. "I think this might be the center."

Lord MacDonald squinted against the sun. "It's worth the time to look."

They angled their horses across the field toward the grove. Her mount snorted again, a single loud canon-like retort in the otherwise still morning. The gelding planted his feet.

Beside her, Gavran's mare rolled her eyes, showing the whites. Her nostrils flared pink, and she tried to turn. Gavran straightened her out.

Ceana prodded her horse with her heels. Lord MacDonald was already at the edge of the clearing, but his horse pulled at the bit. Flecks of foam shot from its mouth, and sweat darkened its skin. She nudged her mount again. He tossed his head and refused to move.

A breeze rattled through the leaves, and Gavran's mare reared, her front legs flailing.

Ceana's gelding shied to the side and bolted. The lurch bent her backward and tore the reins from her hands, burning her already skinned palms. She grabbed the saddle's pommel, her reins flapping loose.

One of the men yelled behind her, but she couldn't catch the words. With every stride, she bounced in the seat. Sparks shot up her tail bone, and her heart punched against the bottom of her throat, making it difficult to catch a breath.

She had to turn the horse around before she traveled too far from Gavran. If she didn't, she'd be sure to fall and break her neck or never find her way back to him or MacDonald castle again.

She dug the nails of her right hand into the leather of the saddle and forced her left hand to let go. At first, she couldn't make it move. She focused and grabbed for the reins. She missed. The reins slapped her mount's neck, urging him on.

She couldn't have more than a few strides left before she'd be out of range.

She made another grab and wrapped her fingers around the reins. She yanked hard to the left, and the gelding slowed and turned in a wide arc. He dropped from a canter to a trot to a walk. His sides heaved.

She slumped in the saddle. Praise be to the Almighty. For once something went right.

She drew closer to the grove. Neither of the other horses were in sight. She swiveled in the saddle. Had she gotten too far away after all? She had no hope if she'd lost Gavran.

A shape she originally thought was a stump straightened up. She shielded her eyes against the glare of the sun. Flaxen and auburn tints in the man's hair caught the light. It had to be Lord MacDonald. Gavran's hair was dark.

Lord MacDonald leaned over another lump on the ground. Gavran.

CHAPTER 18

Ceana urged her horse into a faster walk. She couldn't risk asking him for more and losing control of him again. She stopped him outside the range of where the horses panicked before and slid to the ground. "Is he alright?"

She stumbled over the field's furrows and dropped to her knees beside them. Dirt smeared the side of Gavran's face. She couldn't stop herself from touching her fingertips to his cheek. "Are you hurt?"

"I'll be alright." The white ringing his lips and dark around his eyes said he was in more pain than he wanted to admit. "I never did like riding. Much safer keeping my feet on the ground."

"I think the fall knocked him unconscious for a spell," Lord MacDonald said, "but he'll be fine now."

He grabbed hold of Gavran's shoulders and pulled him into a sitting position.

Gavran grunted and clutched his right shoulder. His face paled to match his lips. His arm dangled at an awkward angle. "Something's off with my arm."

Lord MacDonald prodded Gavran's upper arm and shoulder. "You've snapped it out 'o the socket. I'll put it back in, and we'll have the physician look at you once we return to the castle to see how badly you've injured yourself."

Ceana sat back and covered her face with her muddy hands. She could barely feel the soreness in her skinned palms for the pounding in her head.

There would be costs to this quest. She'd known it. She knew it. If you slaughter a sheep to eat it, you shouldn't be surprised to find your sheep gone from its pen. Yet countless times she'd watched her dadaidh make a desperate, lopsided deal in the market only to regret it the next day, the next week. Perhaps she was more like him than she wanted to own.

A snapping noise, and Gavran screamed. His cry pierced through her ribs and lodged there.

She lowered her hands. Sun filtered through the branches overhead and cast light and shadows across Gavran's face.

When they'd started out, she'd insisted no cost was too high to free her from the curse-side of the wishes. Now she couldn't shake the feeling that not only had she been wrong, but that this quest they were on was a fool's errand that was going to cost her much more than she wanted to pay.

CEANA HUNG BACK OUTSIDE THE CIRCLE OF LORD AND LADY MacDonald and the physician, rocking toe to heel. Her desire to hover over the physician to see that he cared for Gavran and her desire to keep out of his way so he could warred with each other.

The physician fixed a sling of clean material to support Gavran's arm, the elbow bent at a ninety-degree angle. "He'll need to rest the shoulder for six weeks at least."

Ceana released her death-grip on the fabric of her skirt. A timeline for healing was a good sign. "But he'll heal completely?"

"As long as he lets his arm rest, and takes his recovery slowly, he should be back to full strength in a few months."

A few months. Ceana stepped back. All that had registered at first was that Gavran would make a full recovery. She'd ignored how long it would take. Now the words *six weeks* and *a few months* rang clearly in her ears.

Even six weeks was much longer than Gavran had bargained on being gone from his family and their croft when he'd first freed her. Lady MacDonald said Gavran's dadaidh and Tavish still camped nearby and appealed at the castle daily. Every day they waited for Gavran was an extra day Tavish's young sons shouldered the burden of the two families alone. And with his injured arm, even if she released Gavran from his promise and he went home this day, the help he'd provide would be miniscule until near the end of summer.

"What if he uses his arm before then?" Lady MacDonald asked.

The physician nudged his spectacles higher on his nose with the back of his thumb. His bushy eyebrows lowered until they met in the middle.

"Lyall." Lady MacDonald's voice was soft. "This is a matter similar to those you've helped us with before. We cannot wait even a fortnight. What are the real risks of him using his shoulder before it heals?"

The physician ran his gaze up and down Gavran's frame. "You're a farmer?"

Gavran nodded. "Both of the land and a small herd of sheep."

The physician *tusk tusked* with his tongue. "Unless it heals properly, he could spend the rest of his life with it slipping out of place. Unless his shoulder stays in place, he won't be able to plow his land, harvest his crops, sheer his sheep." He snapped his bag shut. "I've warned yeh. But yeh have to be the ones to decide if the risk is one you're willing to take."

Lord MacDonald walked with him out the door. Lady MacDonald sank slowly to her chair.

A chill crept up Ceana's back like ice crystals taking over the surface of a pond. Breaking the blessing of the wishes she'd given Gavran was one thing. It merely set him back to where he would have been before. But this was more. What she'd done to him, what she was doing to him, could leave him worse off than before she'd given him the wishes. Just like her mamaidh and brother were worse off.

"Why can't we wait even a fortnight?" Gavran asked, his voice pulled thin. "You never spoke of a deadline before."

Lady MacDonald folded and unfolded her hands in her lap. "The balance is delicate. The unseelie fae are everywhere. Nothing stays hidden from them long, and you must catch the nuckalevee unaware. Surprise is the one advantage you'll have over it."

Ceana pressed her fingers to her lips and drew in long breaths through her nose. She'd set this in motion. It was what she'd wanted. She'd wanted Gavran to be forced to help her, but now it felt like custard turned to ash in her mouth. "He'll barely be able to lift his arm without pain by then, let alone wield a weapon. And Lord MacDonald will tell you I'm not fit to learn in time."

"You act like I'm the one making the decision." Lady MacDonald flattened her hands on her skirt, as if she realized they betrayed her and she forced them into submission. "Even if the beast itself didn't press our hand, how much longer do you think the people here can endure the tragedy it brings? Look at what it's done in less than a single cycle of the moon."

Once again she was caught between a bad choice and a worse one, only this time she wasn't sure exactly which was which.

Save all those people, including herself. Or save Gavran.

She peeked at Gavran from the corner of her eye. His shoulders slumped forward, and he stared at the floor, eyes downcast. He raised his gaze to meet hers and gave the briefest nod. He was still willing. If she asked it of him, he'd go. He'd risk dying for her. For them all.

Dizziness swirled through her. She wouldn't make this decision alone the way she'd done with the original wishes. This time, she and Gavran would make the decision together as they'd made the decision to fight the nuckalevee in the first place. "We need to—"

The door crashed open. Ceana jumped and spun towards it.

Lord MacDonald stood in the doorway, the hallway dark behind him. His look passed over her as if she weren't there and stopped on Lady MacDonald. "Hugh's arrived early."

CEANA ESCORTED GAVRAN DOWN THE HALL TOWARD HIS bedchamber. Lord and Lady MacDonald had vanished as if chased by the Cù-Sìth.

Gavran shuffled along next to her. With his arm in a sling and his hair sticking up, he looked like a bird with a broken wing. "Who do you suppose Hugh is?" he asked.

They reached his room, and he went inside.

She took one step, two, after him, leaving the door open. "No one good."

He dropped onto the bed. A deep purple bruise now covered the right side of his face.

She eased down to the floor in the corner and pulled her knees up to her chest under her skirt. For the first time, she felt awkward around him. "How is your shoulder?"

He rubbed his good hand along the sling. "The draught from the physician took the edge off."

Tears scalded the back of her eyes. She swallowed them down. Tears would only be seen as manipulation. Whatever decision they made needed to be made unclouded by what he thought he owed her. He didn't owe her anything.

One-armed, Gavran had little hope of surviving a fight with the nuckalevee. Maybe their chances of succeeding had never been great, and it'd taken this to allow her to see it. All she'd seen before was her opportunity to be free of the curses.

She hugged her knees so tight she could have fit in a caterpillar's cocoon. She envied caterpillars. When they disappeared from sight, they came back better, more beautiful. It was what she'd thought she was doing when she gave Gavran the blessing of the wishes. She'd disappear from sight, forgotten, but in return she'd become beautiful inside—redeemed from what she thought she'd done to her brother.

The space inside her chest cavity seemed to shrink to a quarter of its size, and her heart struggled to find room to beat. It hadn't turned out the way she'd planned. Her attempt had left her brother in a worse state than he'd been in before. Now his future and Gavran's future were in her hands again.

She wasn't willing to gamble them a second time on the off chance that a one-armed man and a sickness-weakened woman could defeat a monster. She had to get it right this time. A second chance was rare enough. Third chances came around as often as an eclipse.

They had to wait to fight the nuckalevee until they had the best chance at defeating it. "The wise thing to do is to delay for you to heal. It'll give me more time to regain my strength and practice as well."

A spark ignited in his eyes. It died as quickly as it lit. He looked away. "We have to take the nuckalevee by surprise."

"So says Lady MacDonald, but it's clear she chooses to tell us whatever serves her."

"And all those people?" His lips thinned into unbreakable lines. "We can't leave them to the mercy of the nuckalevee for months."

She suddenly felt lightheaded and suffocatingly warm. In a fair and perfect world, she'd make different choices. But they didn't live in a fair and perfect world. "The MacDonalds could help them, yet they refuse. If we wait, we'll have a better chance of coming out alive and saving my brother. His life matters, too."

Something gave way in Gavran's expression. "Aye, but Lady MacDonald will not easily bend on this."

Ceana chewed the corner of her bottom lip. Buried within Lady MacDonald must be a reason she fought so hard to convince them to go forward. But if she chose not to share her reasons with them, she shouldn't expect them to respect them. "She seems to need us as much as we need her at this point. As long as that holds true, we have something to bargain with."

Gavran nodded and heaved himself to his feet. "We ought to tell her our decision. There's no reason to wait."

CHAPTER 19

L ady MacDonald's pointy-faced guard blocked Ceana's path into the chapel where the wood boy had told them they could find her. "She doesn't wish to be disturbed in her prayers."

Ceana puffed out a gust of air. There wasn't any purpose in aggravating Lady MacDonald. A few minutes wouldn't matter. She sank down onto the stone steps of the chapel.

Gavran perched on the step next to her. "I guess now there *is* a reason to wait."

Ceana nudged his good shoulder with hers and felt the connection all the way down into her soul. This might have been the thing she missed most under the curses—the simple companionship of having someone sit beside her. Of knowing someone cared whether she succeeded or failed. She'd forgotten how it felt.

Movement to her right caught her attention, and she swiveled to face it. One of the gate guards escorted a limping girl into the courtyard and toward the chapel. The girl couldn't have been more than six. Dirt and what looked like blood crusted her bare feet. The way she trailed along behind the guard reminded Ceana of an exhausted puppy dragged on a string.

The guard stopped at the bottom of the chapel steps and looked up at Pointy Face. "We've got another one that needs caring for." He raised a hand beside his mouth as if that would stop everyone else from hearing him. "She walked through the night to make it here. The Death wiped out her whole family."

Behind him, the little girl's fragile shoulders hunched, and her face quivered. Then her jaw clenched and she forced her shoulders back. She stared straight ahead.

Ceana felt it like a punch to her heart, knocking it back in her chest and splintering it into a hundred shards. She pressed a hand to the step behind her. The girl was much too little to have to be that brave. She should have a mamaidh to hold her.

She slid off the steps, knelt in front of the girl, and drew her into her arms. For one breath, two, the girl stayed still and stiff. Then both arms shot up and wrapped around Ceana's neck, tight and frantic, holding on while sobs shook her body so hard Ceana was surprised they didn't break her apart.

She held her back equally tight. She couldn't give the girl much, but she could give her this moment where she didn't have to feel alone.

Pointy Face rubbed his nose with the back of his sleeve and reached for the chapel door. "I'll inform—"

"Her family died of the Death, and you were *eejit* enough to let her in."

The little girl flinched in Ceana's arms, and Ceana clutched her close again. She looked over her shoulder in the direction of the new voice, keeping herself between the girl and its source.

A tall man who looked like he'd stolen Lord MacDonald's nose and chin stood behind Gavran, five feet from the chapel steps. The man wasn't one they'd seen before. With the resemblance to Lord MacDonald, he must be the *Hugh* whose arrival was greeted with such a cold welcome earlier. She could guess why. She'd heard more compassionate tones at an execution.

"Toss her back out before she spreads it to us all," the man said.

The guard closest to her shifted his weight but didn't move towards Ceana and the girl.

"Shouldn't we inform our lady first, sir?" It was Pointy Face who finally spoke.

"My orders don't need agreement from your *lady* to be followed. Remove her. Now."

Anger erupted in Ceana's chest, threatening to boil out of control. Gavran's gaze met hers and locked. He wore his I'm-David-and-this-Goliath's-going-down look.

They rose at the same time. The girl looped her legs around Ceana's waist like a human barnacle.

Almighty save them, the girl probably thought she was going to do as the man asked.

"The only place you're going is to the kitchen for a bannock," she whispered.

The girl's head bobbed ever so slightly against her shoulder.

Gavran planted himself as a barricade between Ceana's bundle and the man. "You can't turn her out. She's a child."

The look on the man's face was one of confusion, like the steps themselves had risen up and spoken to him. For a second she saw them as he must see them. Bone thin. Dirty. Broken. And her in a hand-me-down dress that had once clearly belonged to a woman of a better station.

His expression hardened. "And who are you to tell me what I can't do?"

"They're my guests." Lady MacDonald's voice said from the direction of the chapel.

Ceana shifted her field of vision.

Lady MacDonald stood in the now-open chapel door, her head covering still in place from her prayers. "In a home that belongs to my husband."

The man didn't do anything as obvious as curl his lip, but the tick in his cheek and his darkened eyes said it all.

He turned on his heel and was gone.

Lady MacDonald moved from the doorway, and Pointy Face followed after her, out of the chapel. He must have gone in for her while Ceana was focused on the man.

Lady MacDonald's lips tilted up in what passed for a smile from her. "Thank you, Eachann."

Pointy Face—Eachann—dipped his head.

"You did well bringing her to me," Lady MacDonald said to the other guard. "You may return to your post."

She motioned for the rest of them to follow her.

Ceana shifted the little girl to her other hip. Her arms already ached up into her shoulders, but she wasn't about to put the girl down and ask her to walk on her torn-up feet.

Eachann held out his arms. "I'll carry her."

It was the first time he hadn't looked at her with annoyance or suspicion. Ceana handed the girl over and fell into step beside Gavran.

Lady MacDonald led them across the courtyard, past the stables, to a building that Ceana guessed was the kitchen based on the two girls sitting outside the door on upended buckets, plucking geese and laughing.

They stepped through the doorway, and the aroma of a bevy of spices—garlic, rosemary, mint, root ginger, and so many more —filled Ceana's head. Heat rolled in waves out of the large bread oven and open roasting fires at the end of the room. She blinked against the smoke until her vision cleared.

The kitchen was larger than Gavran's cottage and hers put together. And filled almost entirely with children. Children kneading dough. Children peeling apples. Children straining meat jellies. Even the turnbrochie, rotating sizzling geese on a spit, looked to be younger than the boy who carried wood. He used both hands to turn the spit handle.

Eachann set the girl on top of one of the rough wooden boards balanced on trestles that served as a table. "She's not the first, as you might guess."

Something swirled inside Ceana's chest. She'd been so focused on her goal and on protecting her brother and Gavran that she'd wanted to ignore the bigger picture. Now it stared her in the face in the form of a child—many, many children and more outside the castles walls that she couldn't see.

She'd agreed to fight the nuckalevee for her own sake. She'd wanted to delay fighting it for Gavran's sake. She had to fight now it for the sake of everyone else who couldn't. She had to fight it so that Lady MacDonald could go to her contact and try to keep it from happening again. The unseelie fae couldn't be allowed to continue hurting people without any repercussions.

Gavran tucked in close to her. She could feel him watching her face. "Ceana."

Just her name again, but she knew exactly what he meant. He'd tried to tell her before in his bed chamber that he wanted to fight anyway because more lives were at stake than merely their own. She hadn't wanted to hear him when he said it then, and she'd thrown her brother's situation in his face to stop him. At least she'd recognized her error before it was too late. "I know."

The cook brought clean cloths and a bucket of warm water without even having to be asked. She handed the girl a chunk of bread, nodded to Lady MacDonald, and returned to tying eggs up in a cloth bundle to go into the pot of water boiling nearby.

Lady MacDonald knelt in front of the girl, dipped one of the cloths into the water, and washed her feet. Ceana knew she was staring, but she couldn't seem to look away.

The MacDonalds refusal to fight the nuckalevee made even less sense now. It was clear they cared for the people on their lands. They'd near enough turned their home into an orphanage. And Lady MacDonald washed a poor girl's bloodied feet.

Perhaps they'd just met a clue as to part of what might be driving them. She lowered to the ground next to Lady MacDonald and held out her hand. "Let me help."

Lady MacDonald passed her a cloth. "We'll wrap them up once we finish to help them heal." She smiled up at the little girl, the most genuine expression Ceana had seen from her. "You'll be running again before you know it."

Ceana dabbed gently at the girl's crusted sole. "That man. Who was he?"

"Hugh MacDonald." Lady MacDonald wrung out her cloth. "My husband's cousin. His heir. Should Ihon die without a son, Hugh will inherit Duntulm and its lands."

Anger leaked through in her voice.

A man without compassion made for a hard lord to serve. He'd take from the people until they had nothing left to give, and then he'd still expect more. Lord and Lady MacDonald couldn't risk leaving their people to Hugh MacDonald's mercy because he had none.

Ceana swirled the cloth around in the bucket. Brown and red streaked through the water, muddying it until she could no longer see the bottom. She twisted the cloth long after all the dirty water had drained out.

She'd spent her whole life trying to do something that mattered. Maybe she'd finally found it. "Gavran and I have decided to do as you asked."

CHAPTER 20

Ceana settled in among the remains of a bearberry shrub and rested her bow and *dorlochis* of arrows beside her. The bearberry should have been covered in white, cup-like flowers this time of year, but the blossomless branches sagged, their dark green leaves wilted.

Gavran awkwardly lowered himself next to her using the staff of his Lochabar for support, his right arm in its sling, two days into healing. It was all Lady MacDonald thought they could risk.

"Do you think we'll catch the Black Death from fighting it?" he asked.

He still worried about the consequences of fighting, which meant he still thought they could win this battle. A tiny seed of optimism battled to break through inside her and failed. Gavran had always been the optimist. "We've no way to know."

She pulled out an arrow and scored a line in the dirt. The top layer puffed away, and beneath it, her arrow tip barely made a scratch, like the ground hadn't seen rain in over a year. If they failed tonight, it would be a desert after a year had actually passed. Though perhaps the nuckalevee would move on once it'd killed everyone and everything on MacDonald lands.

Gavran didn't say anything more, and the silence hurt her ears. Not even a mosquito buzzed. The whole grove lay abandoned. The only bird's nest she could spot hung in tatters from the branches, unused. They hadn't broken through a single spider's lair when they pushed through the trees.

What kind of beast could drain the life from an entire grove? Even with all the questions she'd asked Lady MacDonald about the nuckalevee and its abilities over the past two days, she felt nowhere close to understanding it, like she'd tried to plumb the mind of the Almighty. It seemed naïve to believe they could defeat a creature they knew so little about.

A branch snapped, and she nocked an arrow.

"Peace," Gavran's voice came from the darkness next to her. "It was only me."

She'd been so lost in her thoughts that she hadn't even heard him rise. "Where did you go?"

"To look for a better spot." He clumsily edged back down, using a tree and his good arm to guide him. "But there isn't one."

Maybe they needed to look a bit farther out. They didn't

need to wait right on the edge of the clearing. "How far away did you go?"

"I didn't go far enough away for the wishes to cause you any trouble. You didn't miss the nuckalevee because of me." His voice carried an edge.

She hunched her shoulders. "That's not what I meant."

He thumped his head back against the tree. "I'm sorry. Something about this place. It's draining me from the inside."

She felt it, too. Like sorrow and decay crept in through her pores and dried up everything good. If she'd had any doubts they were waiting in the right place, sitting here the past hours had broken them away. This had to be the right spot.

She looked up to where the moon dipped low, already half covered by the treetops. The backdrop of the sky shifted away from cobalt into blue.

It had to be the right spot, and yet the night had nearly passed without a sign of the monster. "It should have shown itself by now."

"We'll have to try again on another night," Gavran said.

They'd achieve nothing by simply sitting out here every night except to exhaust themselves. "We've missed something, and there's no sense in coming back until we figure out what. Why didn't it come?"

"We'll have to ask Lady MacDonald."

"Assuming she'll tell us any more than she already has."

Every time she'd spoken to Lady MacDonald about the

nuckalevee, she had the unsettling feeling there was more hiding right behind the words the lady actually said. Unfortunately, she had no way to prove it and no way to make Lady MacDonald be more forthcoming.

The sun had forced the moon from the sky by the time they walked back to Duntulm Castle. The boy who hauled wood pointed them in the direction of the chapel to find Lady MacDonald. Eachann, as usual, waited outside the door. This time they entered despite his protests.

The chapel stood empty except for Lady MacDonald, morning prayers already done.

Lady MacDonald knelt in front of a stone altar, on the floor like a servant rather than in one of the balconies reserved for the lord's family and honored guests, her covered head bowed. Snatches of her soft prayers carried to the door, magnified by the vaulted ceiling.

Ceana couldn't catch all the words, just their names, and Lady MacDonald's tone—more reverent, more awed and humbled and filled with trust than any prayers she'd heard spoken by a priest. For the first time since the wishes, she *wanted* to kneel down and join in the prayers.

Gavran's heavier footsteps echoed on the stone floor, and Lady MacDonald turned.

The lines around her mouth deepened. She rose and adjusted her head covering higher. It cast her face into shadows. "You didn't fight the nuckalevee."

Ceana glanced down at her mostly clean dress. She guessed it was obvious. They weren't covered in blood, and they weren't dead. "It didn't come. Do you have an answer for why?"

Lady MacDonald seemed to cover the space between them in a blink. She towered over Ceana. The mental image of the fairy towering over her and Gavran stole her breath. She flinched back.

Lady MacDonald drew herself together. She lifted a hand as if she were going to touch Ceana's face, brought it within an inch, but let it fall back to her side. "I'd hoped to avoid what clearly needs to be done."

Ceana opened her mouth to tell her that was no clearer than anything she'd said before, but Lady MacDonald raised a hand again, this time in a *be patient* motion.

"I promise to be less cryptic when I'm sure your ears will be the only ones to hear what I have to say."

She led the way out of the chapel and up the castle stairs. She pushed open the door to a small room with a fire that burned despite the growing warmth of the day. She asked Eachann to wait outside.

Lady MacDonald drew close to the fireplace and held her hands near to the flames. "I can never seem to feel warm until the heart of summer." She turned back to face them. "When you entered the chapel, I was praying the nuckalevee hadn't left you to suffer long before killing you."

Ceana reached out a hand into space but couldn't find

anything to hang on to. They'd been lambs sent to the slaughter after all.

A palm cupped her elbow, and Gavran steadied her.

"So you did send us out to die," Gavran said.

The look on Gavran's face was like that of a dog standing between its master and a wolf. He'd worn that look when she'd run to him, her face bruised from where her dadaidh hit her. It felt like a thousand years since she'd seen that look and struggled to convince him that killing her dadaidh would only see him hung and her family no better off than before. Even after all she'd brought down on him, he still sought to protect her.

Gavran fisted his good hand. "You'll only anger the Lord God Almighty by praying to him and making human sacrifices to demons."

"I'm not fool enough to anger the Holy of Holies." Lady MacDonald spoke the name with reverence again. Like she was awed by merely speaking of God. "I prayed for your quick deaths because I believed you'd challenged the nuckalevee and failed, not because I sent you off to appease the creature's lust for blood and pain."

"And why did you believe we'd failed?" Gavran's tone clearly said he'd need more details if Lady MacDonald expected them to believe her this time.

"We received word at dawn of a new outbreak of the Black Death."

It came, and they'd missed it. Ceana couldn't stop her head

from wagging back and forth. "But we waited at the most likely spot. If you'd seen how void of life it was, you'd be convinced."

Lady MacDonald removed her head covering and folded it into precise squares. "That is my fear. If it avoided its normal spot, it knows we're hunting it, and now it plays with us."

"Then we've no hope of catching it." Hard as she tried to control it, her tone still shot up in pitch, and her words tumbled over each other.

"You've asked that I tell you everything I know about the nuckalevee." In contrast to her own, Lady MacDonald's voice rang hollow. "There's one thing left we can try. We can lure it into a trap with a bait it can't resist."

Ceana's fingers suddenly felt numb. She could think of very few reasons why Lady MacDonald wouldn't have sent them out with bait for the nuckalevee in the beginning. "What do we use for bait?"

"Fresh flesh."

"Then why are we delaying?" Gavran straightened his shoulders. "Have your butcher slaughter a pig."

Lady MacDonald's lips were blue, like cold had set into the marrow of her bones. "Human flesh."

CHAPTER 21

Tremors attacked Ceana's arms, and she gave in to them rather than fighting them. *Monster* wasn't a strong enough term. Gavran had been right when he called the nuckalevee a demon. She suddenly felt naïve for once believing the fairy who cursed them was the worst being out there. At least the fairy had offered good to one of them. "We wouldn't have been enough bait, then? Two of us would have been a feast for it."

Lady MacDonald gave Ceana an I'm-so-sorry-to-be-the-one-to-tell-you-this look. "The flesh needs to be recently dead."

Gavran buried his hands in his hair and pulled. She'd never seen him do that before.

"How recently dead?" She heard herself asking the question, but it felt like the words came from someone else, one part of her detached from the other, like a marionette with frozen strings.

"I can't say."

Ceana tugged her mind back from the corner it wanted to hide in. Lady MacDonald had played with them like a spinning top, keeping them dizzy so they didn't know which direction to face. It was time to stop and hear the whole truth. "You can't tell us more, or you refuse to? What are you still holding back?"

"I can't." Lady MacDonald's words carried a sharp edge. "I may hold more knowledge about the fae than most, but I'm not all-knowing. Only the nuckalevee themselves and the Almighty know at what point dead human flesh stops holding an attraction for them. I've told you all I'm able. I can't even tell you how much flesh would be enough to lure it out."

The implication of what Lady MacDonald had told them clung to Ceana, and the weight of it suddenly seemed to be more than her legs could support. She sank into a chair.

Gavran let go of his hair. "Do you have anyone sentenced for execution?"

"Not at present."

"So all we have to do to trap the nuckalevee is kill someone." His words dripped with enough sarcasm to make the floor slick. "Hunt down a human being like an animal."

Ceana rubbed the spot above her temples where all the tension in the world had pooled. The MacDonalds had no one scheduled for execution, but many people who deserved to die were never caught. Perhaps they could kill someone who deserved to die.

"How could we know who deserves to die and who doesn't?" Gavran said.

Her gaze snapped to him. She couldn't tell if she'd accidentally spoken her thoughts or if he'd merely been thinking the same thing she had. But the question sounded rhetorical, so she must have spoken aloud.

Lady MacDonald held her head covering to herself, crumpling it. There was no more haughtiness or self-righteous anger in her manner. Only sadness so genuine that Ceana wanted to cry. Wanted to cry for her. Except she and Lady MacDonald seemed to share that in common. Neither of them could afford the luxury of tears. They had to hold themselves together. If they broke, the resulting pieces might be too small to find and put back together.

Or maybe she was projecting her own emotions onto the woman because she didn't want to feel alone, now of all times.

"I won't kill someone to lure the nuckalevee." Gavran knelt in front of Ceana, his good hand resting on the arm of her chair. "We have to think about who we want to be when this is done."

Gavran had said as much when she'd suggested killing the spaewife, and he'd been right then, too, even if she hadn't been able to see it at the time. They couldn't kill someone who wasn't part of this.

And yet, making that choice required giving up on saving her brother and all the people plagued by the nuckalevee.

The shivers wracking her moved from the outside in, straight to her center. They were out of options. Her brain couldn't seem to grasp it. "I didn't think this was how it would end."

BLOOD POUNDED IN GAVRAN'S FOREHEAD. HIS LIFE HAD BECOME A fairy tale where everyone ended up losing their heads or drowning in a pot of boiling oil.

He glanced back at Lady MacDonald. "Will you leave us, please?"

Lady MacDonald left without a word.

The ache spread to his heart and wrapped around it until each beat felt like a struggle. He linked his fingers with Ceana's. "We can find another way."

"There is no other way." Her voice had gone flat. "You've said it, and so have I."

He had no answer to that. No good answer, anyway. They had said that. It was the whole reason they'd agreed to fight the nuckalevee in the first place.

She wriggled her fingers from his grasp and stood. She put two steps between them. "It's time for you to go home to your family."

Nae. He moved after her, closing the space between them again. It wasn't fair, nor right. He couldn't let it end this way. He couldn't go home to his blessed life and leave her to the curses once again.

He also couldn't take her back with him. His family wanted her tried for witchcraft. Breaking his promise to Brighde and leaving his family would be more right than abandoning Ceana to her fate. "We can start over somewhere. You'll be safe from the curses as long as we're together."

She smiled as if there were some joke about this that he didn't see. "I thought so, too, at first, but that only works so long as we stay together. There've been so many times I've almost been separated from you already. We could never go anywhere beyond the field borders without the other. Neither of us could have a family. No spouse would abide it."

He ran his hands over the stubble on his cheeks and chin. He couldn't seem to rub away the wrongness of it all. "If you want a family, children, then I'll wed you."

She squeezed her eyes shut so tightly the edges crinkled. "You know as well as I it won't work."

"And why not?"

"You still can't leave me alone. What happens if you have an accident and die? I wouldn't even be able to keep any children alive." She shook her head slowly. "You don't know what it was like with my brother. I won't do that to a child."

The acerbic scent of the smoke from the fire clogged his

brain. He drew a breath in through his mouth and still it choked him. "We can't just give up."

"You tried. We've both tried." Her voice was steady, the deadness replaced by a disturbing calm. "It isn't giving up to stop pushing against a wall that will never topple. It's wisdom."

How could she be at peace with this? He clenched and unclenched his hands, stretched out his fingers, but couldn't get the clenching around his heart to release with them.

She slipped her hand into his and stared down at their linked palms. Her hand hid in his. He'd never noticed before how tiny her hands were. How fragile. And yet she seemed to be facing this situation with more strength than he could muster.

She squeezed his hand. "You always did want to save everyone, and you can't this time, not me or the people here."

He freed his hand and stroked the loose hair back from her face, the face that he'd see every night in his dreams if he left her behind. It was unsettling to be so well-known by someone he felt he'd met but a fortnight ago. If he left her behind, he'd never have a chance to rebuild the friendship they'd had before.

He was also sure he'd never find another like it again. Friendships so deep that one member would give up everything to spare the other couldn't come along twice in a lifetime.

She smiled up at him. "You can still save my brother. With the wishes guaranteeing your success, you can find him and keep him safe. Please do that for me. It's what's mattered to me from the start."

Maybe he'd been trying too hard to find a perfect solution to a situation where there wasn't one and couldn't be one. Maybe this time saving just one boy would have to be enough.

But it didn't it feel like enough.

He wanted to pull her into his arms and shield her, but what he wanted wasn't important anymore. He'd come into this thinking about himself, appeasing his guilt and freeing himself from his dream. If he refused her now, he'd still be thinking about himself.

Instead, he'd go out of it thinking about her. What she wanted and needed was for her brother to be cared for the way he should have been.

"I'll find him. I promise."

"And I know you're much better at keeping them than at making them."

Her smile crumbled, and his heart cracked with it. He pulled the final two coins they'd stolen from his dadaidh out of his pocket and held them out to her.

She accepted them and gave him a firm nod.

He headed for the door, not allowing himself a final look back. He used to think nothing could be worse than dreaming about her every night without an end. Now he knew he'd been wrong.

CHAPTER 22

Ceana stared down at the coins. Enough to buy herself a bannock or two. A day's worth if she could manage to keep it.

Her hands quaked so violently that the coins slipped from her fingers. She dropped to her knees and grabbed for them, but they rolled in all directions. If she couldn't keep hold on them now, what was she to do once Gavran left the boundary of where the wishes and curses canceled each other out?

She slumped forward and pressed her head to the floor. Her chest hurt enough that she should have died from it. But she didn't want to die anymore. She wanted to live a real life again. She'd held it for a moment, and then it'd slipped through her fingers just like Gavran's coins.

The coppery tang of blood flooded her mouth. She eased her jaw and ran her tongue over where she'd bitten the inside of her cheek until she bled without even noticing. She forced herself upright again.

She'd made the right choice, no matter how much it hurt. She'd found a way to ensure her brother would be cared for. That edged her pain in joy. Gavran wouldn't rest until he found him, and Davina's mother-hen instincts would never turn away a young man who couldn't care for himself.

A woosh of air told her the door across the room swung open, and her stomach plunged.

If Gavran had returned, she wouldn't have the courage to chase him away again. He'd almost broken her will when he offered to marry her. He couldn't know how many times before the wishes she'd prayed he would offer. But the wishes seemed to enjoy taking every hope she'd ever had and twisting them beyond recognition.

The footsteps that crossed the room were too light to be Gavran's and accompanied by the rustle of skirts.

He hadn't returned. Lady MacDonald had.

She raised her face.

Lady MacDonald offered her a hand.

Ceana took it. It was a touch colder than her own and reminded her of a breeze passed through a shadow on a hot summer afternoon. "I sent Gavran away with my blessing."

"I saw him on his way out. I instructed him on how to find his father's camp."

"I don't have long until the curses set in again."

Lady MacDonald walked her to a chair. "I've sent for food."

Her stomach growled, and her heart wanted to grab onto Lady MacDonald's kindness and hold it so tightly it couldn't get away, but she couldn't let herself care. Any minute now, whatever she wanted would only turn into the opposite. "I won't be able to eat it."

"You will with my help."

Ceana tucked her hands between her knees. Lady MacDonald must have misunderstood when they'd explained the wishes and curses to her. She didn't have the fortitude to go through it again. Soon it wouldn't matter if Lady MacDonald understood or not.

A servant entered and set a platter of fresh bread, cheese, and ale on the table between them. Lady MacDonald picked up a chunk of bread, added cheese to it, and held it out to Ceana.

Perhaps if she swallowed her food without chewing, she'd get it down before Gavran passed the boundary. She snapped up the bread and cheese and gulped it down.

"You don't need to eat that way," Lady MacDonald said.

Instead of offering Ceana the plate, she handed her another chunk of bread. Ceana hesitated. Lady MacDonald hand-fed her like a mother bird. Something more was going on. How did she put into words what she wanted to know? "The curses—"

"Don't apply to me."

Ceana's appetite vanished. She and Gavran had been right.

Lady MacDonald hadn't told them the whole truth, even after they'd demanded it.

"Take it." Lady MacDonald pushed the food closer. "I can even try handing you the plate to see if it will work."

Ceana took the piece from her hand and chewed it until it dissolved in her mouth. She didn't drop it. It didn't choke her. It didn't bring bile rushing into her throat. "Why is this...? Why am I able to...?"

"I'm immune to fae curses that weren't cast directly on me. If I give you something, you'll be able to use it because I want you to. The curses won't stop you."

Ceana shrank back in her chair. Now that she saw the way Lady MacDonald's hands moved before she spoke, not after, and the quickness of her answers, she could tell Lady MacDonald spoke the truth now and when she said the nuckalevee could only be lured out by freshly dead human flesh. And that she'd lied to them more than once before.

Ceana drew in a deep breath to clear away the weight from her lungs. She couldn't change the past. But this might change her future. "How is that possible?"

A mournful smile flitted across Lady MacDonald's lips. "Call it a blessing that runs in my family line."

"You said you couldn't cure my curse."

"I can't. It doesn't extend far. Only to our direct interactions because it protects me from any influence of your curse."

The clues aligned in her mind like a broken pot melding

itself back together. She must have been blind—or, more honestly, blinded by her own needs—not to have figured it out before. "You're fae. You were fae."

The tightness in Lady MacDonald's figure relaxed, almost as if she was glad to hear it spoken aloud at last. "I was seelie. A selkie. Ihon and I brokered a deal to allow me to stay with him."

"Angering the unseelie. Hence the nuckalevee sent to kill you if you leave your home."

Lady MacDonald nodded. "They feel my permanent presence in the human realm gives unfair advantage to the side of good, despite the restrictions placed on me."

All the things that had bothered her before made sense now. But for one. "The spaewife we met in Dunvegan, how did she know?"

"She's a friend who aided me before I took on a finite human existence. When I became human permanently, I knew the unseelie would seek to harm me and would use anyone I cared about against me. I sent her off to MacLeod lands, the last place anyone loyal to Clan MacDonald would go, to protect her."

There was a resignation in her voice. The tone harmonized with the one deep inside Ceana. Protecting those one loved often required great sacrifices, but one took those on because they valued those lives above their own happiness.

Now she was doubly glad Gavran had prevented her from killing the spaewife.

Lady MacDonald handed her the plate of food.

As she finished off the meal, the gnawing feeling in the back of her mind returned. Lady MacDonald had shown compassion and her desire to protect those she cared about. Yet she hadn't done anything to stop the nuckalevee until Ceana and Gavran showed up. "You lied to us about why you couldn't slay the nuckalevee yourselves."

"Yes." Lady MacDonald's hand fluttered to her stomach. "The seelie and unseelie are at war. If I interfere in that war or attack another fae, Ihon and I will die."

Ceana slumped back in her chair. Emotions tangled up inside her—fear, pity, anger. Mostly anger. All anger.

The anger she'd felt at her dadaidh for wallowing in his grief instead of caring for his family.

The anger she'd felt at the fairy for forcing her into an impossible choice.

The anger she felt at herself for wanting to save herself and Gavran instead of others—Lady MacDonald reflected it back to her, magnified.

She dropped the plate onto the table. It clattered and rolled in a circle. "You allowed all those people to die in order to save yourselves."

Lady MacDonald's eyes turned from brown to black. "You met my husband's heir. What do you think the lives of our people will be like with him as lord? All the children we shelter here would be begging in the streets or worse."

Ceana silently cursed her own arrogance. She'd forgotten about the additional stakes at play. Most people she knew would rather die than live under a cruel lord. Maybe Gavran was right that she was too apt to think she knew best. "I'm sorry, my lady. I spoke rashly."

"Salome."

"What?"

"My name is Salome."

Ceana gave a slow nod. She saw the offer for what it was. Lady MacDonald—Salome felt the same sense of being kindred as she did.

Salome brought her other hand to rest on her belly with the first. "We would both have gladly died to spare them if we believed their lives wouldn't be worse with us gone. If my unborn child proves to be a boy and we can place him safely out of Hugh's reach to grow, perhaps we'll still be able to make that choice before there's no one left to save."

Salome barely showed. Ceana hadn't even noticed the slight bulge until now. She was perhaps four months along, five at most. Even if her child was a boy, their people couldn't survive another four months or more with the nuckalevee roaming free. Even if they did, Hugh might well be appointed to manage MacDonald lands until the child came of age.

But they'd been down this rocky, twisting, barren path before. They needed fresh human flesh to lure the nuckalevee, and then they still needed someone who could kill it.

Black stars burst in her vision, and the noise of her heart beating filled her ears.

Her ragged breathing joined the cacophony inside her head. She wanted to plug her ears, but the sound rolled inside of her.

She knew how to solve the problem of needing fresh flesh. She just wasn't sure she was brave enough to go through with it. Not now when she had peace that her brother and Gavran would be safe.

An image of her brother slid across her mind, followed by the memory of the little girl, her feet bloodied from walking for miles to reach safety, and all the others running around Duntulm Castle. How many more were there dying from the nuckalevee's rampage? How many more that lived but couldn't reach a safe haven? If one of them were her brother, she's want to do whatever it took to save him.

And a death that mattered was better than a life wasted under the curses. Surely it was.

Her heartbeat and breathing slowed. "If you handed me poison, would it work?"

CHAPTER 23

The pounding ache in Gavran's shoulder eased and then vanished, like the last flame sputtering out in a dying fire. He stopped his dragging march toward where Lady MacDonald said his dadaidh and Tavish waited and rubbed a hand over the space where the pain used to be.

The change was...unnatural.

He raised his injured arm above his head. No pain at all. He'd crossed the boundary of the wishes. There could be no other explanation for it. The blessing was back.

Something else was different as well. The air felt easier to breathe. A renewed energy pulsed through his body.

He strode forward. Even walking seemed to require less effort. He covered the ground in less time it seemed.

The cemetery and chapel on the edge of Duntulm soon came into sight. A small swirl of smoke rose above the trees in the distance close to the location where his dadaidh and Tavish should still be camped. It blended in against the low-hanging clouds that drizzled rain onto ground that couldn't seem to accept it.

A wail carried to him on the breeze, and a procession entered the churchyard on the opposite end of the village. Six men bore a long wooden box.

A cadence came from a female figure standing slightly apart —the *bean chaoineadh* leading those gathered in the keening. He couldn't hear the words, but the communal outpouring of grief traveled like waves.

And he felt nothing.

He drank in a breath and laid a hand on his chest. No heaviness. No sense of sadness.

The realization didn't even bring shock, or fear, or any sort of emotion he should have felt. It was all in his mind, and even that grew fuzzier around the edges by the second. He had to concentrate now to hold onto the reason he'd felt sadness before crossing the boundary. It was like grasping at fog on the moors.

He clutched his head. Their plan would never have worked. Before he reached home, he'd have forgotten the blind boy in the market, forgotten Ceana and his promise to find her brother, forgotten all the people living under the tyranny of the nuckalevee. All those memories stolen by the wishes to spare him grief. He'd like as not have eventually accepted his family's claim that he'd been bewitched, and the dreams themselves would cease to hurt him, believed to be no more than remnants of some witch's spells.

Before this day, he'd feared he would feel at least some relief if Ceana sent him home with the wishes intact, and that'd it be yet another sign of his failure to be the kind of man he desired to be. His fear proved groundless, but the reality was worse.

He'd be blinded by his charmed life, not seeing the suffering around him and doing naught to ease it.

He didn't want to live that way, under a so-called blessing that wouldn't even allow him to grieve for the dead.

The dead!

He took two steps forward. A community riddled with death meant dead bodies—some recently dead. A freshly dead body was exactly what they needed.

If he could only make it back inside the area where Ceana's curses cancelled out his blessing before he forgot why he'd wanted to return.

He turned back toward Duntulm Castle and ran.

***

CEANA POURED THE PACKET OF POISON INTO HER CUP AND SET the brown paper aside. It fluttered to the floor. She left it there. When they came to remove her body, it would be a small enough thing for them to remove it as well.

The spoon clinked against the inside of the cup, and the

white powder dissolved into the dark depths of her tea. She raised the cup to her nose and drew in the steam. It smelled like fenugreek and honey.

"You won't taste anything," Salome said. "Would you like me to stay with you?"

Ceana shook her head. She wasn't afraid of dying alone, and the solitude would give her a few moments to make her final peace with the Almighty. Her anger at Him had been as unjustified as her anger at Gavran. All that she'd suffered had made her into someone who was strong enough to make this sacrifice. Perhaps she'd been brought to this point for this very reason. "You've sent someone to fetch Gavran?"

"I will." Salome's voice softened. "Before I do, I want to ask one more time if you're certain. He might choose not to fulfill our request. Some would say fighting the nuckalevee alone is suicide."

They'd already made the choice to fight the nuckalevee if it meant saving the MacDonalds' people. Gavran would have stayed and fought had there been a way to do it without killing someone innocent. She'd provide him a way.

"He'll go."

For a second, she thought Salome would hug her. Instead, she bowed her head. "I'll send Eachann immediately. There are few I trust more." She left.

Ceana turned her back to the door. She brought the cup up to her lips. Her hand shook, and hot tea spilled over, burning her fingers. She set the cup down without drinking it and blew on them. She didn't want to risk sticking her fingers in her mouth and ingesting enough poison to make her sick. That might prevent her from taking enough to kill her.

Red marred her thumb and forefinger, and her fingers pulsed, feeling two sizes too large. Soon burnt fingers wouldn't matter. Soon nothing would matter. All she needed to do was drink the tea.

Taking her life was the better way—the only way.

The poisoned cup stared back at her like a single brown eye. She looked away. Why couldn't she get her hands to pick the cup back up?

Slowly she reached out and wrapped her hand around it. The heat seared her palm. Courage. She clutched tighter and brought it to her mouth. Sweat beaded on her upper lip.

The door swung open behind her.

"I need a little longer," she said. Her voice sounded like a leaf fluttering in the wind.

"For what?"

Gavran. The cup slipped from her fingers the way the coins had and smashed on the floor.

Footsteps crossed the room towards her. Gavran's footsteps.

Or had she drunk the tea already and his voice was a hallucination, part of the poison filling her body?

She turned slowly. He didn't seem like a hallucination, but then again, her experience with hallucinations was limited.

Hadn't Salome left her but a few minutes before? He shouldn't have been here so swiftly. And it would make sense that his face would be the one she saw at death.

Gavran crouched and reached for the shattered pieces of her cup.

She shoved him, and he toppled over. He landed on his injured arm and cursed.

Not a hallucination after all. So it was wise she'd kept him away from her cup.

She held out her palms, facing him, placating the outburst she could see coming. "You might have pricked your finger on the shards."

Gavran lifted his good hand in a *What the hell?* gesture. "Would you have cut off my finger to keep a sliver from growing full of puss too?"

"The tea was poisoned."

He kicked the debris farther away using the bottom of his shoe, his gaze so sharp it would leave a mark. "You meant to kill yourself."

It wasn't a question, but admitting to what she'd intended to do was harder than doing it. It was why she'd insisted Salome wait to bring him back until she had the poison and was prepared to drink.

He crawled to his feet. "You can't keep trying to kill yourself."

"It wasn't suicide this time." She glanced down at the broken cup. "We needed flesh for the nuckalevee. All those people, Gavran, I couldn't—"

He pulled her into his arms and crushed her against his chest.

She wrapped her arms around his waist and clung to him, his heart beating beneath her ear, the same way it had when she'd scraped her knee when she was five and he was eight and he carried her all the way back to her home. It was the day they met.

His Adam's apple bobbed against her hair. "You're an *eejit*, Ceana Campbell."

He said it in the tone someone else would use to say *you're beautiful*. The warmth of his arms, of his voice, made her feel cherished, but she couldn't stay there.

Killing herself was still the best solution.

She pulled away. "You weren't supposed to be here before it was done, but that doesn't change what needs to happen."

"I found another way."

CHAPTER 24

Blood pounded through Gavran's limbs and heart with enough force to burst his veins. If he'd been but a minute later, she'd be gone. Every time his brain came back to it, his blood pressure spiked.

He covered it up with what he hoped was a convincing smile and edged another step further from the stain on the floor made by Ceana's tea. It looked too much like blood.

He motioned toward the door. "They buried someone near Duntulm today. If we hurry, the body might still be considered fresh flesh."

She gnawed the inside of her cheek, a signal he hadn't persuaded her to give up on killing herself yet, though he couldn't explain how he knew. Some part of his unconscious mind still seemed to know things about her that his conscious mind didn't.

"By the time we get the body," she said, "he'll have been dead two days, maybe more."

Stubborn woman. He rubbed his good hand around the back of his neck. "If he's too old, we'll think of something else."

Ceana rocked from her heels to her toes.

He grabbed her hand. She tried to wriggle it away, but he held tight. Finally, she stopped struggling and looked up at him.

Her hand lay limp in his. He stroked the back of her knuckles with his thumb. An emotion he couldn't quite name flickered across her face. The look in her eyes was both fragile and strong.

He didn't want to lose her again, even after all this came to an end. Every night he woke from the dream, he woke missing her.

Where did that leave them should they succeed? His family wouldn't welcome her back. Brighde certainly wouldn't accept her, and he'd made a promise there too—or at least his dadaidh had, and the Almighty commanded him to honor his father.

He gave himself a mental shake. One problem at a time. They might not even live past their battle with the nuckalevee. "Let me help. Let's work together to find another way."

She squeezed his hand. Just enough so he felt it. "It's grave robbing, you know."

"No one will know he's gone, and we won't be hurting anyone. We should try."

"But if the flesh isn't fresh…"

He kept hold of her hand and drew her towards the door. "Don't count troubles afore they come."

———

GAVRAN RELEASED HER HAND AS SOON AS THEY LEFT THE ROOM, and Ceana immediately felt the lack of connection. That hand-clasp had to be the last. Mosquitos who flew into the fire never came out. And they deserved what they got.

She lengthened her stride. "We should take horses. Quicker to ride than to walk, and it'll give us a way to haul the body to the grove."

Gavran groaned. "Aye, if you can stay aboard. I'm like to fall and crack my head this time round."

She wished she could quirk an eyebrow at him, but her eyebrows had never bent to her wishes that way. "I'm taking a man who's afraid of horses to fight a horse-like monster. I don't like my chances."

"So long as you don't ask me to ride the nuckalevee, I'll be fine."

She laughed. It felt a far sight better than crying, and she needed to do one or the other.

Gavran sighed. "Horses it is."

They jogged to the stables.

Gavran went into the door first, looking back towards her. "We'll need shovels. Weapons, too."

Gavran turned back to face forward, stopped. She dodged around him.

Hugh stood inside the stables, his hand on the scruff of a stable boy who looked like Hugh might've hauled him off his feet a time or two already.

The word for the man that jumped into Ceana's mind wouldn't have just made her mamaidh turn over in her grave—she would have died a second time from shock.

"Off with you." Hugh released the lad with a tiny shove, and the boy scuttled away. "There's no good reason for two beggars in my cousin's home to need weapons."

Ceana held Hugh's stare even though she wanted to look at Gavran. Maybe they could bluff themselves through this yet, and looking at Gavran would have implied guilt where there was none.

The moment stretched, but she couldn't come up with a believable reason they needed weapons. She'd been awake for… near a day straight? Seemed like it'd been much longer, but it was only the night before they'd sat vigil for the nuckalevee and failed. Her brain felt mushier than a rotten cabbage.

Hugh's expression darkened. "Rumor amongst the guards is that you're from McLeod lands."

She couldn't stop her gaze from sneaking Gavran's way. He'd done the same, and he had a slightly panicked look in his eyes. Nothing they said would be believed. Not by this man whose pride they'd injured when Salome sided with them over him.

Hugh took up the pitchfork resting against the stall behind him. "I believe you're McLeod spies and assassins."

Ceana's heart thudded in her chest like it was kicking her for her recklessness. They'd become too comfortable in Duntulm Castle with the freedom the MacDonalds gave them. They should have sneaked into the stables or gone to Salome to ask for what they needed, but she'd known Salome and Lord MacDonald would give them whatever they asked for. Asking had seemed like a waste of time. She hadn't considered Hugh.

Hugh pointed the pitchfork at them. "Move."

They backed out of the stables, and he angled them towards the dungeon.

Eejit. Eejit. Eejit. The word kept time with their steps in Ceana's head. They'd handed him the perfect revenge. He didn't even know how perfect. If he locked them away in the dungeon, by the time one of the MacDonalds discovered what happened to them, Gavran's corpse would be long past *fresh*.

"That's alright," Gavran said in a mock whisper. "I'm happy enough to have a dry bed and food brought to me while I rest."

She could have kissed him. If they could goad Hugh into kicking them out of Duntulm Castle instead of locking them away, they'd at least still have a chance. "Aye, without the horses, it'd be a long walk back to Dunvegan."

"To the left," Hugh said from behind them. "You're not headed to the dungeon. We're headed to the gates."

Praise be to the Almighty. Hugh's desire not to feed "beggars" or "spies" seemed stronger than his common sense. Now they just needed to figure out how to find weapons and, if they survived the nuckalevee, sneak back into a castle from which they'd been exiled.

GAVRAN PARTED THE BRANCHES OF THE TREES SO HE AND CEANA could better see the graveyard. He bit back a curse. The gravedigger had already finished and gone.

When he watched the funeral procession earlier, he'd tried to take careful note of where the new hole lay, but he hadn't had time to wait and mark the spot for fear his memories would fade too much for him to remember what he needed to do. He'd assumed that they'd also have the aid of making it back before the gravedigger finished his task.

Up close, more than one recently-dug grave looked like it could have been in the place he noted from his distant vantage point earlier, and the downpour had made it near impossible to tell which had been filled this day and which earlier in the week.

He touched Ceana's shoulder, and she jumped. "We still need shovels."

"We'll have to borrow one." She trailed along after him. He heard more than saw her scuff the toe of her shoe into the ground. "Assuming we make it through this alive, what will you do once we break the wishes? Will you return home and marry Brighde?"

He blew a long breath out through his teeth. A week ago, he would have said aye. His dadaidh made an agreement with Tavish, and he wasn't going to ask him to go back on his word. But without the wishes, everything would be different. He was already different.

"I don't know. Doesn't seem fair to hold her to it when she might not have wanted to marry me if I hadn't been blessed by your wishes. We weren't promised before, were we?"

Ceana's upper body became unnaturally still. "You weren't promised to anyone, despite half the families in the kirk wanting you for their daughters."

"Sure enough you're exaggerating." Though perhaps not. He never lacked for partners at a dance or supper. "If I had so many fishing for me, why hadn't I let one catch me?"

Ceana kept her profile to him. A pulse beat a flutter at her temple. She didn't answer.

They came over the top of a hill, and she pointed ahead to a darkened cottage. The yard was deserted except for a single chicken scratching in the grass and two sheep that looked like they wore more wool than meat on them.

"Let's find the shovels," she said.

They slunk through the yard and peered into the lean-to. Only one shovel.

Gavran picked it up. "Should we keep looking for another?"

Ceana nodded and wove her way across the yard toward a small barn. "It was because of me."

He glanced back at the cottage. Still no sign of movement. Either they didn't have a dog to warn them of trespass or the family had been wiped out by the Death. "What was because of you?"

"I think...I think you hadn't married because you felt you needed to care for me, and you knew you wouldn't be able to once you had the responsibilities of your own wife and bairns."

He jammed the tip of the shovel into the ground. In the dream, he'd told her it was past time she found someone to care for her. Trying to remember his dream in detail, though, was like trying to speak a language he'd never learned. He couldn't hope to know his past motives. If the feelings that clung to him like echoes now could be trusted, however, what he meant was he wanted to be the one to care for her—permanently. "If I did, it was my choice, and I don't regret it."

She tugged on the barn door. The rickety structure trembled, but the door held. "You can't say that. You might have. My dadaidh always said I was a burden."

She spoke the last words softly, as if it were an admission of guilt.

He couldn't even imagine what having a dadaidh like that did to a person. Maybe it explained why she was so willing to throw her life away. "We all need help sometimes."

She yanked on the door again, and it flung open. She ducked inside.

"Found one." She emerged from the barn holding a shovel with a broken-off handle. "Do you think it's worth taking?"

At least they'd have a backup if the whole shovel broke. "Best we get out of sight before they wake or return."

DARKNESS PUSHED THE LAST THREADS OF PURPLE AND RED FROM the sky, and the new moon hovered low, seeming to struggle to rise. The lanterns in the church were finally out, and the buzz of mosquitoes had replaced the drone of late-evening flies.

Shovels in hand, they picked their way across the slippery graveyard. If his mamaidh was wrong and ghosts did haunt the graveyard until the next funeral, this man would sure enough come back to plague them while they stole his body.

Ceana stopped at the edge of the rectangle of bare earth. Her brow furrowed. "Is this the right one?"

Gavran squinted, but blackness blocked his view past where Ceana stood. He laid the shovel aside and went further into the graveyard. His feet sank into another plot of soil recently dug. "There's another here that looks fresh. How do we tell which one is his?"

Ceana joined him, her broken shovel still in hand. "Maybe it doesn't matter, as long as they're both recently dead."

He dug into the dirt with the toe of his boot. "With all that rain, could be this one's already a week beyond. I'm certain a fortnight won't count as fresh."

Ceana motioned towards the interior of the graveyard. "I'll check some of the others. You're sure it was around here?"

"Aye. It was this side of the church, by the break in the fence. It has to be within the first two rows." He knelt and scooped up a hand of dirt. It clumped in his fingers, almost holding its structure. He went back to the other plot and did the same. The clump felt looser. He rubbed it between his thumb and forefinger, and it smeared, more mud than dirt. "I think this is it."

"I see a few others that look recent, but none that look newer than those two." Ceana's voice floated on the darkness like a specter.

"Then we'll have to take a chance."

She appeared at his side. The wind kicked up, wailing through the trees in a mimicry of the keener's cry. "Do you think we can catch the Death from the body?"

He'd asked her almost that very thing about the nuckalevee, and he had no better answer to give. "I've no idea how it spreads. We'll have to pray the Almighty protects us." He pushed the shovel into the earth with his foot and dug up the first scoop, carrying the weight of it on his good arm. "Sooner started, sooner done."

Ceana dug her broken shovel into the ground beside him. She was short enough she didn't even need to bend over to use it. The scratch and plop of shoveled dirt gave him something to focus on other than the wind rattling through the branches near them.

They removed layer after layer of dirt and sunk into the ground.

Ceana stopped and leaned on her shovel. She wiped an arm across her brow, breathing heavily. "I'm sorry. I'm still so weak."

They couldn't be more than a few inches from the coffin now. He punched his shovel down again and hit something solid. "We're nearly there. You rest while I clean the top off."

She climbed out and dropped into the grass next to the plot. He scraped the remaining inches of dirt from the lid of the coffin and laid the shovel up on the edge of the hole.

Ceana peered over the side. "How are we going to get him out? I'm not strong enough to haul him up on my own or to lift him up to you."

Gavran rubbed a grimy knuckle across his chin. The grains of dirt scratched his skin. "If you can hold him in place long enough, I'll climb out and help you drag him up."

She flopped down on her belly, her arms hanging over the edge.

He drew a slow breath and wrapped his fingers around the lip of the coffin. He pried at it, ignoring the searing pain in his injured shoulder. The lid didn't budge. Nailed shut. "Toss me a shovel."

She lowered a shovel over the edge. He raked moist dirt from the side to give himself more room for leverage and wedged the shovel tip under the lid. He leaned back on the handle, and the lid groaned and then cracked. The sound bounced out of the hole, off the church, and ricocheted over the fields. He flinched.

Ceana glanced backward. "Do you think anyone heard that?"

Most people would be asleep. If the noise woke them, no one was likely to connect it with a violated coffin. He peeled the board back with his hands, and it broke.

A stench worse than rotted vegetables hit him in the face. He stumbled back and choked down the bile burning his throat. Above him, Ceana gagged and rolled away from the hole.

He held his breath and leaned over the gap in the coffin lid. The stiff, bloated face of a woman stared back at him.

The sound of retching from up top stilled, and Ceana's pale face appeared at the edge again. "It's not the right grave, is it?"

He shook his head. However long this woman had been dead, she was well past fresh flesh.

"What do we do now?" Ceana's voice shook.

The moon had managed to creep its way directly overhead of them. "We still have time. We'll dig out the other grave. It must be that one." Gavran rubbed his aching shoulder. Assuming the strength in his arm held out that long. Grave-robbing wouldn't be on the physician's list of approved activity for his shoulder any more than wielding a Lochabar was. "I need to rest a bit first, though."

Light skittered across the right side of Ceana's face. Her head snapped in the direction of the source, and a curse fit for a dock-worker slipped from her mouth. She reached down, not looking in his direction. "Get out. Quick."

He seized her hand with his good left one. "What's wrong?"

"The priest is coming."

The light swayed as if the priest were running, and a holler loud enough to raise the village ruptured the otherwise quiet night. She leaned back, and his toes scratched the edge. He tumbled on top of her and rolled to the side.

The lantern light hit him straight in the face, blinding him. As the light swung away and his eyes adjusted, he glimpsed a burly man brandishing a lantern in one hand and a thick staff in the other.

Ceana grabbed his hand and half helped, half hauled him to his feet. They left the shovels beside the hole and sprinted from the graveyard without looking back.

"I've seen you," the priest yelled after them. "I know what you look like. You'll be called to account for this desecration."

CHAPTER 25

The pressure in Ceana's chest felt like she had to cry or she wouldn't be able to breathe. Like the tears needed to come out or they'd flood her lungs, drowning her.

But she'd rather stop breathing, rather drown, than allow herself to cry. Hadn't her dadaidh beaten it into her that crying never changed anything?

She sat shoulder to shoulder with Gavran in a patch of scrub brush far enough from Duntulm that the villagers wouldn't find them on their torch-and-pitchfork hunt.

Gavran snapped a long blade of grass between his fingers. "Do you think he thought we were fae? The priest, I mean."

"Why would fae rob a grave?"

Gavran shrugged, barely more than a jiggle of his shoulders.

She let the silence fall again. They needed to talk about what would happen next, with no flesh to lure the nuckalevee. But for a few minutes more she wanted to pretend like they had another choice and rested here to catch their breath before pursuing it.

"How much do you think we need?" Gavran's voice was rough.

He could mean only one thing, but she didn't want to answer him. "Flesh?"

His head dipped once.

Was a nuckalevee like a shark who couldn't resist a drop of blood in the water, or more like a wolf who'd need an entire fresh carcass before it'd risk coming out into the open? Given the way the MacDonalds described it, it was like to be more ravenous shark than skittish wolf. And while she'd been willing to die for this, she'd much rather lose only a part of herself. "Not a whole body, if that's what you're asking."

He snapped the blade of grass so hard it broke. "An arm then, or could we get by with a hand."

It'd been the same thing she wondered since the priest ran them off. She could survive with one hand. It'd limit the work she could do, but the MacDonalds surely wouldn't turn her out after all of this. Her marriage prospects were nil since the wishes anyway, so losing a hand, or even an arm, wouldn't leave her any worse off in that area than before.

There was one problem. "If we take only the hand, and it's not enough, then we've cut off the hand for nothing."

The weak moonlight reflected off Gavran's face, making him pale as an albino. He gave a sharp nod. "The whole arm then."

A chill carried up her fingers and into her arms. She tucked her hands under her armpits. He'd agreed to that easily. He'd proven that he wasn't indifferent or selfish, so that couldn't be the cause. It must be that she'd intended to kill herself earlier. Perhaps he was simply glad she'd agreed to a lesser butchery.

He climbed to his feet slowly, stiffly, reminding her of an old man. He plodded out of their hiding place.

She scrambled after him. He headed in the wrong direction. "Where are you going?"

"MacDonald castle. We'll need an axe."

They'd be eejits to waste a day walking back to MacDonald castle, not to mention the obstacle of getting back in since, on their way out, Hugh ordered the gate guards to bar them entry, and the MacDonalds didn't know of it. "We can steal one, same as we did the shovels."

"The priest raised the whole village over us violating the graves." He ground out the words. "And we'll need to cauterize the wound with something hot."

His irritation seemed out of proportion, but, then again, Gavran'd always been a touch short-tempered when exhaustion hit him. They were both far past exhaustion. Let him have it his way. Her brain already felt full of sheep's wool and spider webs, so she wasn't the best judge at the moment.

Their feet crunched across the dry grass, and to their left, wind swirled the loose soil up into funnels like it hadn't poured rain only hours ago. In the near perfect dark, the funnels looked like angry spirits rising from the ground to chase them.

She shook herself but couldn't clear the feeling. It must be the silence of the walk. "Feels like a storm coming."

"You'll need to tie the tourniquet tight."

She tripped and righted herself. He was still thinking about what they had to do. "Aye."

"With the arm gone, there's a risk of bleeding to death otherwise."

And infection. And shock. She clamped her teeth together as if that would block off the thoughts. No sense in ruminating on them like a goat on old cud. This had to be done. They needed flesh. "Won't you take care of that? The tourniquet."

His eyebrows dipped down, darkening his eyes, and he gave her an are-we-talking-about-the-same-thing look. "How do you expect me to tie it on my own arm?"

She stumbled back a step. "What do you mean *your* arm? I thought we were going to cut off *my* arm."

"That's why you didn't argue with me." He spoke the words slowly, drawing them out as if processing the idea as he said them. Relief and something else she couldn't identify warred with each other on his face. "I thought you didn't care if I chopped off my arm, and I started to think maybe I'd been…" He shook his head. "It doesn't matter what I thought. I was wrong."

She pressed a fist over her mouth and closed her eyes. He

hadn't disagreed with her because he hadn't realized what she meant to do. "I thought you weren't arguing with me because of how I've berated you when you didn't give me my way. And because I offered to sacrifice my whole self before."

When she opened her eyes again, he had the kind of half-committed smile on his face that said *I'm not sure I should find this funny but I do.* "Have we always been like two bairns learning to talk when it came to communicating?"

She smiled to give him permission to joke about it. His half smile grew into a full one. It was so easy to forget that he didn't remember their history. All the times they'd fought and reconciled, debated and come to a compromise. "We did tend to assume the other person knew what we meant, and so we oft ran ahead, thinking we were on the same path when we weren't. We always figured it out eventually."

Almost always. Neither of them had broached the topic of their relationship before the wishes. They'd been the best of friends, as close as family, and there were moments when she thought he wanted more. She'd catch him looking at her lips. He'd choose her company over that of other women at community events. But neither of them spoke about it. Her hints went unanswered.

And then it was too late.

She pulled her shoulders back into a no-argument line. Enough dwelling on the past. He had no memory of what once was, and they had bigger problems now. "We're not cutting off your arm."

"We agreed a hand might not be enough. And if it isn't, I've lost my hand for nothing."

She had no intention of chopping off any part of him. "No hand, either. How do you expect to fight the nuckalevee one-handed? If we cut off a part of one of us, then it should be me. I'm the weaker fighter, and if this doesn't work, I'm worthless anyway."

She wanted to grab the words back as soon as she'd said them. It was the type of thing she would have said before the wishes, always trying to get Gavran to confess some feeling for her beyond a brotherly affection and giving him opportunities he never took. Hadn't she just told herself they were past that?

She smoothed the strands of her hair whipped loose by the wind and their run through the woods. "What I mean is that if we don't defeat the nuckalevee, Lady MacDonald can't help us find a cure for the wishes. I'm the one who stands the most to gain, so I should be the one to lose something in return."

"Haven't you lost enough?" The lines in Gavran's forehead deepened. "Let me give something up for you."

Her breath suddenly seemed thick in her lungs, like trying to breathe pudding. "You've given up plenty. You just don't remember most of it."

Gavran clasped her upper arms and stared down into her eyes. "Do you have to argue with everything I say?"

For a second, she allowed herself to pretend none of this had ever happened. That they were standing in the woods near home, arguing over whether Gavran would chop wood for them or she'd continue collecting sticks. She stamped down on the flutters in her belly, crushing the life from them. Treacherous body.

She ducked away from his touch. He insisted he be the one to sever a part of his flesh, and she refused to take it. They'd reached an impasse.

She kicked at a nearby rock, missed, and smashed her toe into the ground. Pain shot up her foot, and she cried out.

Gavran frowned. "What did you do?"

"Stubbed my toe again. You'd think I'd have learned not to kick at rocks by now with all my battered toes." She jerked her head up. That was it. "A toe. We could cut off a toe."

Gavran had his lips pressed into a firm martyr's line. "We don't know that will be enough."

"But if it's not, I've only lost a toe, the littlest one."

"It'll be my toe." His eyes turned vulnerable, almost pleading. "I want to do this for you. I might not have anything to prove to you, but I still have something to prove to myself."

Gavran couldn't have known it was the same look he'd worn the day Davina shattered her knee, when he came for her in the middle of the afternoon and begged her to help them.

The day she'd abandoned her work repairing their fishing nets and went with Gavran, even with her dadaidh, too drunk to walk, screaming after her that she took better care of strangers than of her own kin and it'd be her fault when they had nothing to sell at market.

The day she'd spent the night caring for Davina and returned home at dawn to have her dadaidh take a rod to her back for being a whore and swear that he'd never let Gavran Anderson have her even if he begged and offered their whole herd in exchange.

If Gavran had given her that look and asked her to run away with him, she would have stolen her brother in the night and gone. But he never asked.

Instead, he asked that she allow him to be the one to cut off his toe.

And, even now, when he gave her that look, she couldn't tell him *no*.

CHAPTER 26

The guard door slammed in their faces.

Ceana planted her hands on her hips. With the day part gone, the guards at the gate were the ones who'd been there when Hugh evicted them the day before. They might have had a chance had they been able to make it back to Duntulm Castle before the night guards retired. The current guards refused to even deliver a message to Salome.

Salome must have noticed her disappearance by now, but without knowing Hugh had barred them from the castle, she wouldn't be aware of their situation or even certain that they hadn't simply abandoned the quest and run off.

"Should we wait for nightfall and hope they don't pass on Hugh's orders to their replacements?"

Gavran rubbed his palms around the back of his neck and stretched out his back. His eyes were bloodshot. "Aye, makes sense. But we'll need food and water soon enough. And sleep, too."

Sleep they could nab anywhere. The other two were less likely. Ceana considered kicking a rock by the side of the road but thought better of it.

"Down." Gavran grabbed her wrist and yanked her off the road. "Someone's coming."

She ducked behind the trees and peeked out. The dust cloud took shape into a mounted figure.

Gavran leaned his head against the tree trunk beside her. "Only one. It's not my dadaidh and Tavish."

Ceana squinted. It wasn't Allan or Tavish, but she recognized the figure. "It's Eachann."

She stepped back out onto the road and waved her arms. Gavran joined her.

Eachann's mount broke into a trot and stopped next to them. He glared at Gavran. "Where've you been? Lady MacDonald said I should fetch you from your dadaidh's camp, and when I got there, they'd not seen you. I've been searching all night."

Eachann's horse snuffled Ceana's hair. She ran a hand down the animal's sweaty forehead. "Plans changed."

"Well, his dadaidh and his companion are out hunting all round Duntulm for him now. They're a feared something terrible happened."

Kicking that rock looked more appealing all the time. With Allan and Tavish actively seeking Gavran, it made it that much more likely that they'd stumble across them before they were able to kill the nuckalevee and make it back to Duntulm Castle.

Eachann nodded towards the gate. "Come along inside. Our lady is probably worried enough herself by now."

If they went in, the guards were sure to report to Hugh, forcing a confrontation between Hugh, Salome, and Lord MacDonald and causing more delays. Aside from that, they didn't need attention drawn to what they were doing at Duntulm. Hugh was the last person they wanted knowing about the nuckalevee or suspecting Salome's true nature. He hated her enough already.

Ceana took hold of his mount's reins. "Hugh MacDonald's forbidden us entry to the castle."

"He's been angling for that since you stood up to him about the girl I'd imagine." Eachann spit on the ground. "No matter. I'll bring you in myself. He's no right to toss out people given sanctuary by the lord and lady."

How much to tell him? Salome said she trusted Eachann, and yet her true nature and the existence of the nuckalevee seemed to be secrets she kept from even her most trusted. Her secrets weren't theirs to share.

But they still needed aid. "We can't go back in now without causing trouble for Lord and Lady MacDonald, and we've been given a task by Lady MacDonald. We need your help to complete it."

Eachann's eyes narrowed. "What kind of help?"

He didn't know them. He had no reason to trust them, either. "Supplies only." She glanced at Gavran, and her stomach dipped. She didn't know if she were strong enough—physically or emotionally—to cut off his toe herself. "And perhaps help with a small task."

Eachann gaze moved between them. He stiffened and sat back in his saddle.

Gavran's lips twitched in that struggling-between-a-smile-and-a-frown way, as if he wasn't sure whether to be amused by the pun of *small* or annoyed that she referred to cutting off his little toe as a small task. "Take our request to Lady MacDonald, tell her where we are and why. That way you can be sure you're fulfilling your oath."

Eachann loosened his horse's reins. "Fair enough. Tell me what you need, and I'll return before the sun sets." He shooed a fly away from his face. "And get some rest while I'm gone. You both look like death."

CHAPTER 27

Gavran limped beside her, his face still gray as cold ash.

Ceana laid a hand over the tiny lump in her pocket where his smallest toe lay wrapped in a piece of cloth torn from Eachann's tunic. Sickly tasting saliva flooded her mouth, and she wrenched her hand away.

She'd stayed by Gavran's side, let him crush her hand while Eachann sliced off the toe. The leather belt Eachann gave him to bite down on had barely muffled his scream. Gavran hadn't even had a drink to dull the agony for fear it'd dull his mind when it came time to face the nuckalevee.

Her vision spun slightly. She needed to focus on what came next. If she kept thinking about Gavran's toe, she wouldn't make it to the grove, let alone have the balance and strength to help fight the nuckalevee.

She peeked at Gavran from the corner of her eye and tried to think of happier thoughts, but everything she could come up with was tinted with sorrow.

Gavran held back the branches along the edge of the grove, and she stepped into the deadened clearing again.

She edged to the center, sliding sideways to keep Gavran in sight, and shoved her hand into her pocket. She closed her fingers around the cloth bundle, pulled it out, opened her hand. It was like someone else was doing it all and she watched from a distance.

A small red stain on the cloth marked where his toe continued to bleed after they wrapped it up. At least it was only the smallest toe. She had to keep repeating that to herself.

She knelt down, turning her back to Gavran and shielding the toe from his vision. She fought against a shudder and rolled the toe off the cloth onto the ground.

She focused her gaze on the tree line, stuffed the cloth back into her pocket, and went to the bushes where she'd last seen Gavran. A rustle told her where he was.

She waded in and settled beside him. "How long do you think it will take?"

Gavran shifted his Lochabar to the side, giving her more room. "It should be quick. It likes the"—he glanced at the foot that was one toe short—"flesh fresh."

The skin on her arms broke out into goose pimples. So if it

wasn't here by the time the moon was near to its apex, they'd know a toe wasn't enough.

Gavran gazed intently into the center of the clearing, a frown creasing his forehead. "I think we're going about this wrong."

She refused to look in that direction. "It's a little late for that, don't you think?"

"I didn't mean *that*." He nodded his head towards where his toe lay. "I mean we shouldn't both attack it from the front."

It made sense, but to have to sit alone in the dark and wait for a monster... "I think we should stick together. What if I get too far away from you?"

"You won't. This clearing's nowhere near large enough. Just stay inside the tree line."

With her luck, if she argued with him longer, she'd be caught in the open when the nuckalevee showed up. She picked up the second Lochabar, the one Eachann brought not knowing she needed a *dorlochis* and arrows instead. In their exhaustion, they hadn't been clear enough about what weapons they needed. At least before he'd cut off Gavran's toe, he'd sawed off the Lochabar's shaft to make it a better height for her.

Even though it was a longer route, she skirted the edge of the clearing rather than going straight across past Gavran's toe. She ducked behind a drooping scaly fern.

The foliage gave her the perfect amount of cover. She could see out, but wouldn't be immediately obvious to a creature coming in. Lady MacDonald said it would be sudden. She'd blink with the clearing empty and, when her eyelids lifted again, the nuckalevee would be there.

Was it wrong of her to hope it faced Gavran and she could come at it from behind? Even with his injured shoulder, he was more skilled than she was with the Lochabar. It'd take months of training, not days, to change that.

She settled in and slowed her breathing. If she sounded like a panting dog on a summer day, she'd scare the nuckalevee away before she had a chance to strike the first blow.

Her hands felt like she'd dipped them in ice water. She rubbed them together, then wrapped them around the Lochabar's staff. How long had it been? The moon hardly seemed to have shifted position in the sky. What if it didn't come? The toe might not be enough to draw it.

She dug her nails into the wood of the staff. If the nuckalevee would just show itself, it'd be better than waiting here, unsure of when or if it was ever going to arrive.

The wind shifted and bore the stench of putrid flesh straight into her face.

Bile seared her throat. She clamped a hand over her mouth and gagged it back.

That wasn't coming from Gavran's toe, was it? The stink was even viler than the body they'd dug up. The only time she'd ever smelled anything like it was when she'd stumbled across a dead animal that must have been too sick for even the carrion animals to want it, its flesh melted in the sun and maggots spilling from its eyes.

Her eyes stung, and she blinked rapidly. Her vision cleared.

A creature twice the size of a normal horse pawed the earth in the center of the clearing. Black blood flowed through veins and arteries exposed to the air, and its bloodless muscles rippled and twitched like a fish when filleted freshly caught.

This was it. This was the nuckalevee.

It lowered its head and sniffed Gavran's toe, inhaling so deeply the white bones of its ribs stretched. Again and again it breathed. Somehow she'd expected it to eat it. But this was worse. A lust for blood and pain was how Lady MacDonald described it. It seemed to feed on the pain and fear still clinging to the amputated digit.

She swallowed, but her mouth was parched, and her throat wouldn't work. Why didn't Gavran charge it already? She couldn't kill it alone. She couldn't kill a moth alone.

Gavran sprinted across the opening. She fumbled to get a firm grip on her Lochabar. It slid through her damp palms.

Gavran drove toward the nuckalevee, but it slipped to the side like Gavran was moving in slow motion. It twisted around to face him.

Because she'd been too slow, they were now on the same side of the clearing again.

"Ceana!" Gavran yelled.

She plunged through the underbrush, running parallel to the

nuckalevee, an arm up to protect her face. Branches slashed her chest and arm. Surely it could hear her, but she had to try to get behind it again. She burst from the bushes across from the nuckalevee's right flank.

The nuckalevee kicked its front hoof out at Gavran in a way no natural horse ever could. He threw his Lochabar up in front of it, and the nuckalevee's blow shattered the staff in half. Another blow like that and he'd have nothing to defend himself with.

She drove forward, aiming her Lochabar at what looked to be an organ at the back of its belly. The nuckalevee pivoted to face her.

Its eyes were haunted gold like a cat's, not the red or brown she'd expected. Prepared herself for. She wasn't prepared. They weren't prepared. They could have never been prepared no matter how long they waited, how many questions they asked.

She rammed her Lochabar straight into the nuckalevee's chest and bounced backward. The Lochabar flew from her grip, and she crashed into the ground. Hot pain raced up her spine, and her hands and feet went numb. Sensation came back in fragments.

The nuckalevee stayed planted in place. Her Lochabar hadn't even nicked its flesh.

It lowered its head and weaved its neck like a snake, its mouth open. It exhaled, and a dirty gray mist curled around her. Her eyes felt filled with grit and her lungs burned.

She sipped in shallow breaths, but the ache in her chest spread. The ground seemed to shimmy around her, and the withered grass under her fingers crumbled and swirled away. The nuckalevee's outline was blurry through the haze.

Then it spun away, and the mist evaporated. She collapsed flat to the ground, gasping. Gavran's form pitched what she could only guess were rocks at the nuckalevee.

She scrubbed her eyes. They watered up from the pressure, and tears streamed down her cheeks, clearing out whatever poison it was the nuckalevee shot at her. Her Lochabar was gone, heaved into who knew what part of the undergrowth.

They were going to die.

The nuckalevee kicked out at Gavran again. He ducked and rolled, but the blow connected with his shoulder. He cried out. The nuckalevee struck again, barely missing his skull. Gavran came up holding his broken Lochabar.

She crab-crawled backwards to the edge of the tree line. She had to find a branch or something she could use as a weapon. Gavran dodged to the side, moving closer and closer to where she lay.

She dragged herself to her feet, using the nearest tree for leverage. Another toppled tree wedged into the V of its branches. She leaped, hands in the air, reaching for one of the low-hanging limbs of the dead tree. Her fingers didn't even brush the bark.

She scoured the nearby ground cover. All the fallen wood

was no bigger than firewood kindling. Everything bigger was either out of her reach or too large for her to break from the tree.

"You need to run."

She whirled around. Gavran crouched an arm's length from her. He swung at the nuckalevee, and it danced a step backwards.

"I'll find my Lochabar or something else I can use. I'm not abandoning you."

Gavran panted, his face red and sweat streaming from his forehead. "I'm not asking you to. You have to get far enough away so the wishes and curses don't cancel each other out anymore."

Of course. Once she was far enough away, he'd be able to defeat the nuckalevee thanks to the power of the wishes. "But I won't be able to find you after."

"Head in the direction of Duntulm Castle. I'll find you. Go."

The nuckalevee swung towards her, its golden eye staring unblinkingly at her.

"Go, Ceana. Trust me." Gavran shoved her in the direction of the bushes. "It's our only chance."

CHAPTER 28

Ceana sprinted into the underbrush. The thick branches grabbed and clutched at her clothing and hair like they served the nuckalevee, trying to hold her in place. A branch sliced her cheek, and warm blood slipped down her face. She dashed it away and plowed forward.

How far did she need to go? She'd never asked Gavran how far away he actually went the night she drank the spaewife's brew and they tested to see if the wishes had broken.

Gavran's scream echoed behind her, and she skidded to a stop. She turned back. She shouldn't leave him to face it alone, but he was right—their only hope of defeating a supernatural monster was to use fae magic against it. And the only fae magic they had was the wishes.

She looped her skirt up into the belt around her waist and, bare-legged, ran as hard as she could away from the clearing. She had to get far enough away before the nuckalevee hurt Gavran so badly he couldn't fight.

THE NUCKALEVEE'S FRONT HOOF GOUGED THROUGH THE SKIN across his ribs.

Gavran tried to bite back the scream but couldn't hold it in. Each blow felt like stinging nettle rubbed into an already ragged wound. And he'd swear on the holy book the monster grew stronger with every blow, like it was feeding off his agony.

He dove into the underbrush, ducked under a low-hanging branch, and ripped the sling off his injured arm. The sling made him clumsier than he could afford. If he was to have a chance of hanging on until Ceana ran far enough away for the power of the wishes to return, he couldn't afford anything slowing him down.

He rolled back out into the clearing. The nuckalevee seemed to track his movements even when he couldn't see it and reared up directly in front of where he landed. He jumped to his feet.

The nuckalevee charged. Its shoulder clipped him, and he corkscrewed through the air. He smashed into the ground on his injured shoulder. Daggers of pain trembled through his body like a mild seizure. He staggered upright. He had to hang on a little longer.

He glanced over his shoulder at the underbrush. How determined was the nuckalevee? Was it defending itself because they attacked it, or would it have attacked them if he hadn't struck first? Based on what it'd done to the people and land, he'd guess it wouldn't simply disappear if he gave up the offensive and made himself harder to reach.

The nuckalevee charged again. Instead of trying to dodge it, he leapt behind a tree. The nuckalevee slammed chest-first into the truck.

With a boom like a cracking stone, the trunk snapped. The tree groaned and swayed, then tipped slowly back.

He scrambled out of the way of the branches. It toppled into the trees behind it, and leaves rained down. The nuckalevee shook its head as if disoriented. Blood gushed from a gash above its eye.

The trick wouldn't work again, but now it'd be half blinded by the blood at least.

Gavran shifted the broken Lochabar to his injured hand. His hand trembled, and he had to concentrate to close his fingers around the staff.

The nuckalevee turned toward him again. He grabbed a low-hanging branch of a young whitebeam tree with his good hand and jumped. He landed belly-first on the branch and swung one leg over. Branch by branch, he crept up the tree. The nuckalevee paced in front of his perch and snorted like a thunderclap.

Maybe Ceana was far enough away at last. Now he needed to figure out where the monster might be vulnerable.

CEANA DOUBLED OVER AND VOMITED FROM HER PROLONGED sprint. Her stomach heaved long past emptiness, and her lungs ached.

She had to keep running. Keep running until she hit Duntulm Castle, if that's what it took. At least Gavran would think to look for her there if he managed to survive.

She forced her legs to move into a jog. The ground seemed to shift underneath her, buckling and folding. She lost her footing and tumbled back the way she'd come. She crawled to her knees, then back to her feet.

She scrubbed at her eyes. The ground in front of her was flat as a table and twice as level. Exhaustion and thirst must be making her dizzy enough to trip over her own feet.

She loped forward again and again the ground appeared to rise up, creating a slope too steep to climb. She slid backwards, grabbing at grass. It ripped from the ground, and she somersaulted feet over head.

Her heart quivered in her chest like it might stop beating. This could be only one thing. She'd reached the edge of the boundary where Gavran's wishes canceled out her curses, and because she wanted to stay past it, she couldn't. One step beyond was all it took, and when the curses gained control, they threw her back.

Which meant Gavran wouldn't have more than a few

seconds at a time of the wishes' power, and he'd only have those for as long as she could physically keep bashing herself against the boundary.

THE NUCKALEVEE WHIRLED AND KICKED THE TREE WITH ITS BACK hooves. Shockwaves rippled up the tree, and the branch Gavran straddled bounced. He slipped to the side, grabbed the tree trunk, and lost his grip on the Lochabar. It tumbled to the ground. He hauled himself upright again using the trunk. His fingernails were torn and bleeding, but the pain throughout his body had become so all-consuming he couldn't tell if his actual fingers ached or not.

He wrapped his arms in a bear hug around the trunk, and the nuckalevee kicked again. The tree's trunk snapped and groaned.

Something was wrong. If Ceana made it far enough away that the wishes became active again, he shouldn't have lost his hold on the Lochabar. And the tree he rode shouldn't have been creaking, its trunk about to surrender and send him careening through the other trees.

He swung down a branch. The nuckalevee struck again, and the tree tilted and crashed into another tree. Gavran pitched sideways, his grasp slipping. He dangled from the branch by his good arm. The bark scored his palm.

The nuckalevee's hindquarters heaved in another kick.

Gavran swung forward, then back, and pushed off the tree trunk with his feet. He plunged down and grabbed on to a lower branch of the nearest tree. His good shoulder burst into flames with the impact, and his already-injured shoulder sent searing heat licking out through his back and up his neck.

He hooked his armpits over the branch. The pain eased and almost disappeared, then returned again in a fresh blaze. It was almost as if the wishes flickered like a candle, helping guide him one minute, then snuffing out under a strong wind. Whatever the reason, if he was right, he'd only have moments at a time.

The pain ebbed again, and he dropped down two branches. When it returned, he paused to breathe. The nuckalevee redirected its attack to the new tree.

The tree shuddered beneath him. He hung over the edge for a clearer look at the monster.

Lord MacDonald warned them not to underestimate it. Its hide might look vulnerable with its exposed veins and muscles, but it was more impenetrable than the castle walls. If the outside of the beast was hard like armor, perhaps the only vulnerable spot was inside, inside its jaw and up through its brain.

The nuckalevee bucked against the tree, but this time the trunk didn't even wobble. Gavran slid the rest of the way to the ground, snatched up his Lochabar, and sprinted back into the open center of the clearing while he still had the protection of the wishes.

The nuckalevee stalked after him, but slowly, picking each

step with the care of an animal who knew traps were set. How intelligent was it? Lady MacDonald seemed to think of it as if it had human-like intellect, but Lord MacDonald spoke about it more like a blood-crazed beast.

The nuckalevee stopped well out of reach of his Lochabar, even if the staff wasn't half its original length. It opened its mouth, and the same gray mist it shot at Ceana earlier rolled out.

His lungs convulsed, and his throat closed. He had to hang on until the next time the wishes took over.

The mist tightened around him, and the nuckalevee closed on him. Saliva dripped from its fangs.

He fought to swallow and failed. Black spots teased across his vision, and his legs morphed into punky wood, bending when they should have stayed straight.

The nuckalevee's gaping jaw was almost within arm's length now. If Ceana could give him one more opening with the wishes...

His lungs opened, and the mist was more like breathing in normal fog than gas from a sulfur pit. He wrapped both hands around the staff of his Lochabar, leaped forward, and jammed it through the roof of the nuckalevee's mouth.

CHAPTER 29

Ceana pressed her sweat-soaked forehead into the grass. Running had quickly turned to jogging, then walking. If she wanted to charge the barrier again, this time it would have to be on hands and knees. Her whole body quivered. Surely Gavran had killed the nuckalevee by now. But if he had, why hadn't he come looking for her?

Unless he was dead.

A gust of air chilled her damp skin. She lifted her face to the sky. The stars had faded. Dawn wasn't long from coming. The nuckalevee wouldn't stay in their world once daylight came. She had to go back and find out if she'd given Gavran enough time to kill it or not.

She pushed up to one knee. To her feet. There'd be no running back, and if the nuckalevee were still there, feasting on Gavran's corpse, she'd be its next meal.

She dragged herself forward one step at a time, stubbing her toes and tripping with near every step. Her body ached in a way she'd never experienced, not even after the beating a fishmonger gave her for trying to steal roe from a gutted fish after she hadn't eaten anything in four days.

Red and yellow tendrils crawled up from the horizon line, and a kestrel's squa-ua-ua jarred her ears. Two mounted figures broke the smooth hilltop to her right.

She dropped to her belly in the long grass. She didn't need to catch anyone's interest and have them follow her. A wounded or dying Gavran would be hard enough to explain, a nuckalevee's body near impossible.

The figures cut across the hillside. Something about them looked familiar.

She waited. They moved out of the back light of the sunrise. Allan and Tavish. They still stood watch for him.

She crawled forward, low to the ground. It'd take her twice as long to make it back this way, but she couldn't risk them spotting her. She wasn't in any shape to evade them if they recognized her.

Rocks bruised her knees even through her skirt and tore at her palms. She couldn't see how far she'd come, making it feel like she edged her way through an endless tunnel. Perhaps she did. If Gavran had died, the wishes would have her in their clutches once again. Forever.

Shade stretched over her and she looked up. The trees of the nuckalevee's clearing towered above. No sounds came from inside. The fight was over, and either Gavran had left to look for her or...

She stood and forged her way into the clearing. The nuckalevee's body lay crumpled at the far side, a Lochabar spike poking up through the top of its skull.

She swayed and grabbed a low-hanging tree branch. Gavran did it. He must be out looking for her. While she waited, she'd see if there was some part of the nuckalevee they could cut off and take back to Lord and Lady MacDonald as proof. She wasn't taking any chances.

She shuffled across the clearing. A grin stretched her lips and filled her heart. The people here were safe, and in a matter of days, she'd be free of this curse. Perhaps once she found her brother, Lady MacDonald would hire her to work in the kitchens of the castle. That wasn't too much to ask. She'd always been a fine cook, able to make much from a very little, and they could no doubt use another undercook to supervise all the children.

The nuckalevee's stench triggered her gagging reflex again, and she breathed through her mouth. Not that she had anything left in her stomach to heave.

The beast's golden eye stared emptily toward her, and a sticky looking stream of blood pooled under its cheek...and around a boot.

Her vision tunneled down. The trees vanished, even the

nuckalevee vanished. All she could see, all she could think about, was the boot.

Gavran wouldn't have left his boot behind.

She tried to force her legs to walk forward, but they refused.

The nuckalevee was dead, but if Gavran were dead as well... Nae, he couldn't be. She'd managed to come back here, which meant the wishes and curses were still canceling each other out. He had to still be alive.

She careened forward and skirted the nuckalevee's corpse. Gavran lay crumbled on the ground on the other side, leine stained with red.

She dropped to her knees and pressed her fingers to his lips. A shallow breath pulsed against her skin. Very shallow.

She tore open his leine. A wound gaped up over his ribs and across his chest, nearly exposing the bone. Bits of dried blood formed an imperfect crust, oozing around the edges. He wasn't dead, but he would be if she didn't get him to a physician.

"Help! Help me!"

She clamped a hand over her mouth. She'd forgotten that the nearest souls likely to hear her were Allan and Tavish. They wouldn't take him back to the MacDonald's castle. They'd take him home, away from her. *If* they allowed her to live after all they believed she'd done. Maybe they'd string her up from one of these trees for witchcraft.

She had to get Gavran into the bushes where she could hide him until she figured out how to bring him aid.

She scuttled around behind him, and looped her arms under his armpits, pulling him tight to her chest. His head flopped back against her neck. His skin scorched hers. Blood soaked through the front of her dress, hot and sticky. Was he bleeding from the back, too? There was too much blood.

She tilted her head so that her cheek rested against his forehead. He wasn't going to make it. Even if she managed to get him back to the castle in time and into the care of the MacDonalds' physician, he wasn't going to make it. No one recovered from wounds this severe, setting aside what further damage the nuckalevee had done inside. Each breath she took still burned like swallowing boiling water thanks to the nuckalevee's poison mist.

She ran her fingers through his hair, down his jaw line, and suddenly it was like watching the life they'd spent together played back in front of her eyes.

Gavran planting their fields, long after the sun left the sky, his back already aching from helping his own dadaidh, when hers passed out drunk. Gavran standing at their door, snow clinging to his hair, with a smoked mutton in his arms the long winter they almost starved. Gavran paddling through the water, dragging her dead weight behind him and refusing to let her go, the night he came to bring her in from collecting cockles and they almost drowned.

The warmth of his smile and the loch-blue of his eyes and the way he said her name and how safe it felt to be held by him.

Pressure built in her eyes. She dug her nails into her palms deep enough to bruise, fighting against the tears, but they pushed their way out, unstoppable, carrying the force of all the times she'd wanted to cry in the last fifteen years and hadn't allowed it.

Breaking the wishes meant nothing if Gavran died.

She had to draw the attention of Allan and Tavish and let them take Gavran away from her. The wishes would take over again. They'd heal him. It was his only chance to survive. She'd endure the cursed side of the wishes if it meant he'd survive. If given the choice a thousand times, she'd always choose to save Gavran over herself.

Because even when she'd hated him, she'd never stopped loving him.

She eased away from him and lowered him to the ground as she would have laid a bairn in its crib. She pressed a kiss to his forehead, his eyelids, his cheeks.

And, finally, gently, to his lips.

She slid his *sgian* out of its sheath and tucked it into her belt. If Allan or Tavish spotted her, brandishing a weapon at them might be her only chance of escaping.

"Help!" She screamed as loud as her poison-burned lungs could handle. "Someone please help!"

This time the beat of galloping hooves sounded clearly in the distance. She hid in the bushes.

Allan and Tavish burst into the clearing on foot. They stuttered to a stop, and Tavish gaped open-mouthed towards the nuckalevee's corpse. She could only imagine what they were thinking. She'd been prepared to face a monster when they camped out in the clearing. The men responded to a call for help and stumbled upon a monster.

"What is it?" Allan asked. His voice carried the tone of someone who'd walked onto the scene of a fatal accident and whose mind couldn't comprehend the tragedy before them.

Tavish swore low under his breath. Ceana couldn't hear the invectives, but she knew the sound.

They drew their swords and parted, creeping up on either side of the nuckalevee.

Ceana flattened herself to the ground. She must stay invisible. They had to find Gavran and focus on saving him rather than on hunting her.

Tavish cursed again. He dropped to his knees next to Gavran's form. "Allan, it's Gavran."

Allan's sword sagged, and he sprinted around the nuckalevee. He ripped a strip off his leine and applied it to the wound in Gavran's chest. "He still breathes."

"You don't think…" Tavish poked the nuckalevee with his sword. "You don't think this is the girl, do ya?"

Allan smoothed a hand across his sun-wrinkled forehead as if trying to press the wrinkles out. "It must be. He broke the hold she had on him, and she showed her true form. It was worse than we thought."

"What do we do with it? We can't leave it here. What if it's not full dead and hunts him down?"

"We have to burn it."

If they burned the corpse, she'd have no proof for Salome that they'd killed the nuckalevee at all. Ceana compulsively picked at the dirt under her fingernails, the need to move rushing through her body and finding release in the only avenue that wouldn't give her away. What if the MacDonalds didn't believe her?

"We won't be able to carry Gavran out on horseback," Allan said. "While you collect wood for the fire, I'll build a sling. If we can bring him to Duntulm, we can send for a physician from there. I won't take him back to that castle. From the way she protected the girl, Lady MacDonald might've been in league with the monster all along."

Allan bound Gavran's chest wound and carried him away from the nuckalevee. Together, Allan and Tavish chopped two large branches from a tree. She could only guess that Allan planned to use them to build the sling so they could haul Gavran to Duntulm behind one of the horses. Allan disappeared out of the clearing and returned with a blanket. Tavish foraged the tree line, building a pile of sticks in the center of the clearing.

If she was going to salvage any part of the nuckalevee, it had to be now, while their backs were turned.

She wiggled on her belly like a snail through the undergrowth until the nuckalevee's corpse lay between her and the men. She pulled the *sgian* from the belt at her waist and clamped the antler handle in her teeth. She needed to cut off a part that would be small enough to sneak away with yet was obviously part of the nuckalevee.

A hoof could as easily belong to a large horse, and she'd not be able to saw through the iron-hard flesh and bone with a *sgian*. Gavran had stabbed it through the mouth, so she might be able to cut out the tongue, but that might not be distinctive enough.

She shut her eyes, and the image of the nuckalevee turning its glowing golden eye on her sent a tremor down her back. The eye. It had to be the eye.

She peeked out of the brush but couldn't see either man. She crawled forward. Her knees and elbows felt like they were on fire. Crawling forced her to drag her own dead weight. One body length, two, three. She arrived at the nuckalevee and slowly twisted its head back so that its eye faced her.

Even though it was dead, the eye still seemed to look through her, down into the dark parts she didn't want to think about. Calling to them. She plunged the *sgian* into the edge of its eye socket.

With a squish, fluid gushed from the socket, and she fought back a shiver-start.

She sawed the *sgian* around the edges and levered the eye. It popped out and hit the ground, nerves and black goo trailing around it. A whiff of freshly sheared wheat hit her, so different from what she'd expected and from the stench that hung over the nuckalevee in a cloud.

She reached out for the eye but recoiled. It was one thing to pop it out and another thing entirely to have to touch it.

"I have enough." Tavish's voice reached her from across the clearing. "But she'll be too heavy to drag over here. We'd be better to pile the wood around her."

No more time to be squeamish. She grabbed the eye and shoved it into the purse where she'd carried Gavran's toe on the way here. The eye felt slimy, like a jellyfish.

She squeezed her eyes shut for a second. No different than a jellyfish. No different than a jellyfish.

She jabbed the *sgian* back into its sheath and skittered on hands and knees into the underbrush.

She cleared an opening in the dry leaves just big enough to see out of and curled herself into a ball.

Allan and Tavish stacked wood on top of and around the nuckalevee. The fire caught and began to crackle. They hauled Gavran from the clearing, and she was alone with the flames and, soon, with the curses.

She limped out of the bushes and skirted the clearing, wiping sweat from her brow from the flames. She waded through the trees on the far side. Tavish held the reins of Allan's horse, and Allan walked beside the sling carrying Gavran that dragged behind his mount.

She watched them until they disappeared out of sight. Any

minute now the curses would take over again, and she wouldn't be able to do what she wanted.

She held the *sgian* away from her at arms' length. The nuckalevee's eye seemed to pulse in the pouch at her waist, and the thought flitted through her head that she still had time. She could kill herself before the wishes took over again rather than taking the risk that Gavran wouldn't come back for her and she'd be trapped. Maybe that risk was too big.

This time, though, it was one she was going to take. She wasn't going to be like her dadaidh who always talked about change and never acted on it. She'd decided to trust Gavran. She'd decided to let someone else help her rather than trying to control everything herself.

Once he was well, he'd keep his promise and come for her. In the meantime, she had to find a way to return to Salome's side, send him a message letting him know she still lived, and hold on long enough for him to come for her. He'd asked her to trust him, and she would. This time, he'd remember her when awake. This time, he'd find her on purpose.

It was her only hope. And, for the first time, when hope tried to resurrect, she didn't bind it like a sheep for slaughter and slit its throat. She let it take hold and grow.

She pulled back her arm and heaved the *sgian* into the midst of the flames surrounding the nuckalevee.

She'd take one problem at a time until she either reached Salome or Gavran found her. The first was she wouldn't be able to get to Salome directly. Even if she acted quickly, she'd only be running farther away from Gavran, making the curses take control more swiftly. Yet as long as she sat here and the only thing she wanted was to reach MacDonald castle, she ensured she'd never make it there.

The nuckalevee's corpse belched plumes of black smoke into the sky, and the air around her cracked with dryness and rained soot and cinders down on her head. She ought to leave the clearing while she still could, in case the flames leapt to the dead trees and bushes and burned the whole clearing to the ground.

At least since she wanted to go to Duntulm Castle, she should be able to reach the town of Duntulm for the night.

CHAPTER 30

Ceana left the clearing, and wind bashed into her. She bowed her head and drove forward. No wonder the nuckalevee fire accelerated into an inferno. The small breezes making their way through the trees from the more intense wind outside the clearing would have stoked it like a bellows.

"You there," a man's voice yelled. "Stop."

Ceana spun around. Two men slid their horses to a stop an arm's length from her. Dirt kicked up into the air. She lifted an arm and shielded her face against the swirling debris.

The taller of the men sat his horse warrior-straight, his face as unreadable as blank parchment. The squatter man bared his yellowed teeth at her. The right front tooth was missing, making him look simultaneously fierce and funny.

The taller man pointed towards the blazing clearing. "What kind of an *eejit* leaves their cook fire burning when the trees around are like tinder?"

Egged on by the wind, the nuckalevee's fire had indeed spread to the nearest trees. Perhaps it was a blessing the men were here. With the parched grass all around, a fire could rage out of control. At least it would have devoured the nuckalevee before anyone else saw it. She didn't relish being accused of meddling in dark magic again. Especially not without Gavran around to buffer the curses.

"What do you have to say for yourself?" the tall man asked.

They thought she'd lit the fire? "Nae. It wasn't a cook fire, and I—"

"You set it on purpose then?"

She shook her head, but he leaped from his horse and grabbed her by the arm. She was an *eejit*. She'd forgotten how adaptive the curses could be. The instant she'd set her goal on reaching Duntulm, she'd guaranteed she'd never cross the boundary past the first home.

The tall man hauled her closer to Gap-Tooth. "She fits the description the priest gave of the two who was robbing the grave the other night."

"Aye." Gap-Tooth's words whistled on the way out. "And now she's here causing more trouble."

She squirmed in the tall man's grip even though it wouldn't

do any good. Because she wanted to escape, she couldn't. Gavran might come back for her, but who knew if she'd be alive when he did. "I didn't set the fire."

The tall man squeezed so hard she had to bite back a whimper.

"Then who did? You're the only one I see around here, and we saw you coming out of the clearing, plain as anything. And you weren't running for help to put it out, neither."

She clamped her lips shut. There was no point in arguing. It wouldn't do her any good. Sometimes, if she acted swift enough, she could get out in front of the curses by a second or two, but there was no doing that here. No getting away. No convincing them she wasn't trying to burn down the whole countryside.

Gap-Tooth shifted in his saddle as if he wasn't sure whether to stay mounted or join in interrogating her from the ground. "Nothing to say for yourself now?"

"Toss me a rope," the tall man said. "I'll take her to answer for her crimes. You head back for help to put that blaze out."

Gap-Tooth tossed down a rope, and the tall man caught it in the air with one hand, never letting her go. He whirled her around and lashed her arms behind her back. She didn't bother to struggle.

"You ought to cover her eyes, too," Gap-Tooth said from behind them. "No telling why she was robbing those graves. Might be for some devil-worshipping ritual, and you don't want to take the risk she can curse you with a glance once you're alone with 'er."

The tall man grunted assent, pulled a dirty rag from his pocket, and tied it around her eyes. It reeked of sweat and rancid duck fat.

Something shoved her forward, and she stumbled. The heat of the fire snapped at her face. Her arms were tugged up, and her shoulders felt like they'd burst from their sockets.

"You're fortunate I'm a God-fearing man, or I'd toss you into the flames. Whatsoever a man reaps, that also shall he sow."

She bit her lip to keep from crying out. She'd allowed herself to forget too much. What made her think she could reach any place she wanted to go once Gavran was out of range? And now, because she didn't want to be tried for a crime she didn't commit, she'd have no way to escape it.

The man lifted her off her feet and dropped her over a sharp, furry mound that smelled like horse and leather. It had to be his horse's withers.

Blood rushed to her head. The animal shifted beneath her, and a bulk settled in behind her. Rough hands jostled her into a sitting position.

She focused on clearing her mind, but thoughts of coming before someone who'd decide she should be lashed—or worse—for the fire tore at her mind like a starving beast. She didn't want it, and yet she knew it had to be coming.

The horse lurched forward, and she clenched her legs around it. Even though the man's arms boxed her in on either side, he wasn't likely to care if she fell.

The horse broke into a trot, and she bounced around, her teeth jamming together, unable to get her balance with her hands behind her back. Would she fall off because she didn't want to, or would that smaller failure be trumped by the larger one of losing her freedom?

The soft plopping footfalls of hooves on grass turned into the heavier clop of hard-packed earth. They must have reached the town. Nae, they couldn't be in Duntulm. That's where she'd been headed. But if they weren't in Duntulm, where had he taken her?

She wiggled her forehead and opened and closed her jaw, but the blindfold stayed in place over her eyes.

The horse stopped, and the man drew away his arms. Without the bracing, she slid to the side. She smashed into the ground, and her head bounced off the hard earth. Buzzing filled her ears, and heat rushed through her body.

Fight it. Fight. It. She had to stay conscious.

She blinked against the rough blindfold. It'd slipped down enough in the fall that she could catch motion around her. Voices droned like a swarm of angry hornets, but she couldn't focus enough to make out the words. She sucked in air through her nose and pushed it out her mouth.

It was no use. Blackness deeper than any blindfold could provide overwhelmed her.

———

SOMETHING COOL AND DAMP BLOTTED AT HER FACE. SHE LICKED her lips. Her dry mouth tasted like she'd eaten coal, and her eyelids were unusually heavy. She squirmed and forced her eyes to open to slits.

A shadowy form hovered over her. "Easy. You're safe."

A woman's voice. Familiar. But it couldn't be.

She opened her eyes fully. Salome perched on the bed next to her.

She was safe. "How?"

A single word at a time seemed to be all her brain could manage around the throbbing in her head.

"A man from Duntulm brought you here to have you thrown in the dungeon on the charge of setting fire to the countryside. My lord husband recognized you and called for me." She stroked back Ceana's hair. "Did you kill it?"

Ceana slid her hand underneath the covers to her purse. The bulge of the nuckalevee's eye was still there, though it felt flatter, like she might have crushed it in her fall. "Aye."

"And Gavran? Why wasn't he with you?"

"Gone."

Ceana's eyes felt too heavy again to keep open anymore. She

could explain it all to Salome on the morrow. They'd send a message to Gavran, and then she'd wait while he healed.

She brushed her fingertips against her lips. Last time they'd parted, she'd given him the dream to remember her.

This time, just in case hope tried to fail her, she'd given herself the kiss.

LETTER FROM THE AUTHOR

Authors sometimes talk about books they had to write because they fell in love with the story and the characters. This is one of those books for me. I originally came up with the seed idea for *Cursed Wishes* back in 2013, and I've been waiting ever since for a chance to write it.

One of my favorite things about the story was the idea of wishes where two people had to receive opposite results. I wanted to play with the idea of what that would mean and what the relationship between the two people would be like.

Broken Wishes (Book 2) releases later this year, as does Lady MacDonald's origin story *Stolen Wishes*. If you'd like to know when they're available, the best way is to sign up for my newsletter at www.subscribepage.com/threewishesstory.

My newsletter subscribers receive *Three Wishes*, the prequel short story, as a welcome gift. *Three Wishes* shows exactly what happened the night Ceana and Gavran received the wishes.

If you liked *Cursed Wishes*, I'd also really appreciate it if you took a minute to leave a rating. Ratings and reviews help me sell more books (which allows me to keep writing them), and they help fellow readers know if this is a book they might enjoy.

Until next time!

Marcy

ABOUT THE AUTHOR

Marcy Kennedy is a science fiction and fantasy author who believes there's always hope. Sometimes you just have to dig a little harder to find it.

In a world that can be dark and brutal and unfair, hope is one of our most powerful weapons. Hope is the certain expectation that something better is coming if we don't give up.

She writes novels that encourage people to keep fighting. She wants them to know that no one is beyond redemption and that, in the end, good always wins.

She also writes award-winning mysteries under a pen name, but that's a secret. Shhhh…

Marcy lives in Ontario, Canada, with her former Marine husband, human-sized Great Dane, six cats, and budgie. In her free time, she loves playing board games and going for bike rides.

She loves hearing from readers.

www.marcykennedy.com

authormarcykennedy@gmail.com

84579453R00188

Made in the USA
San Bernardino, CA
09 August 2018